"I'm
unco... ...ional, Nathan began.

She had no experience with marriage, conventional or
otherwise. "I intend to be a good wife, Nathan."

"I appreciate that," he replied. "Everything is new to you. The
territory. This marriage. Because of the circumstances, we
were forced to make decisions quickly, and that's not an ideal
condition. Courting gives a couple time to learn about each
other, time to grow comfortable and at ease."

"I don't feel cheated," she said. "I'm prepared to be your
wife."

* * *

Her Wyoming Man
Harlequin® Historical #1047—July 2011

Author Note

Summer is my favorite time of year. There's nothing like a lazy summer day spent with a sweating glass of iced tea and a good book. Whether you're vacationing or at home, at the beach or inside with your air-conditioning, I hope Ella and Nathan's story sweeps you away and gives you hours of reading enjoyment.

I'd love to share one of my favorite summer recipes with you. Several years back I bought a fistful of handwritten recipe cards at a flea market, all of which were obviously quite old.

RHUBARB COBBLER
From the kitchen of Gladys

Place 4 to 6 cups of cleaned and chopped rhubarb in 9-by-13-inch pan (lightly sprayed or not). Sprinkle with ¼ cup (or less) sugar.

Cream together all at once:
¾ cup (or less) sugar
1 cup flour
3 tbsp melted oleo (margarine)
½ cup milk
1 tsp baking powder
salt

Pour batter over rhubarb.

Mix 1 cup (or less) sugar with 1 tbsp cornstarch. Sprinkle over batter.

Pour 1 cup boiling water over all. Grind cinnamon over the top. Bake 30-35 minutes at 350 degrees.

CHERYL
ST. JOHN

Her Wyoming Man

TORONTO NEW YORK LONDON
AMSTERDAM PARIS SYDNEY HAMBURG
STOCKHOLM ATHENS TOKYO MILAN MADRID
PRAGUE WARSAW BUDAPEST AUCKLAND

Recycling programs
for this product may
not exist in your area.

ISBN-13: 978-0-373-29647-7

HER WYOMING MAN

Copyright © 2011 by Cheryl Ludwigs

This story is dedicated to Kristin
with appreciation for everything from getting up with me
during the night to making me eat and doing my laundry—
oh, and for always keeping the teapot full.
I couldn't have been bionic without you.

Chapter One

Dodge City, Kansas, April 1873

The maid guided Ella's familiar gentleman caller into the dining room. Ella offered him her gloved hand and he held her fingers briefly, his smile unusually stiff, before pulling out her chair. His demeanor signaled a warning; but she didn't allow her curiosity or concern to show.

She seated herself at the table elegantly set with gold-trimmed dishes and sparkling silver, where five other couples were already absorbed in their own conversations and flirtation.

"The sky was especially pretty today," Ella said, her flawless French accent as natural as drawing breath. "It was a lovely afternoon for reading on my balcony."

"It's a nice evening, as well," he replied.

He'd called twice a week for the past three years, and still their dinner conversation centered on the weather and other trivial topics. She understood that he was married, though he'd never mentioned his wife's name or anything about his family. Ansel Murdock was probably in his middle to late forties, held a stockholder's position at the livestock exchange and belonged to a gentleman's club as well as the local Episcopal Church.

But on Monday and Friday evenings, he visited Ella—or Gabrielle Dubois, as she'd been known by and referred to since she was ten years old.

They ate their roasted duck and steamed asparagus, but when the mousse was served, she sipped coffee while he enjoyed his delicious-looking confection. She had never been served a dessert, though she'd managed to sneak a taste or two when no one was looking.

At last the meal was over and a maid served sherry in tiny crystal goblets. Ella most often carried hers upstairs to enjoy later. He accompanied her now, his unfamiliar impatience unnerving. He was always a gentleman and never in a hurry.

She locked them inside her room and set her glass on the inlaid table that sat beside a plush fainting couch. "Would you like me to wind the phonograph? I have a new Edison cylinder."

"Gabrielle, I have some difficult news."

She posed on the deep blue velvet upholstery, artfully arranging the folds of her yellow tulle gown.

"What is it, Ansel? Are you ill?" She masked her concern before a frown could crease her brow.

"My health is excellent. But the fact is, I am relocating.

I have an opportunity I can't pass on, and well, my wife wants to move back East now that our boys are off to university."

Her heart sank at his news, but she kept her expression pleasant. "Oh, I see."

Mr. Murdock retained her exclusive attentions. Because of his generous monetary hold, no other revenue was expected of her. Once he was gone, she would be assigned a new gentleman. And if the new man wasn't rich enough or willing to retain her exclusively, more than one caller would be required.

As though he sensed her thoughts, he said, "You're young, Gabrielle. You are by far the most beautiful woman in all of Dodge City and most likely Kansas, for that matter. You won't lack for attention."

How well she knew. There had been many inquiries, but Mr. Murdock's retention kept those other companions at bay. "You're right of course. I do hope your move is beneficial for all concerned."

Cordial, never defensive, always congenial and favoring male opinions and desires, those were her ingrained behaviors. Neither the dozen concerns flashing through her mind or her precarious future were reflected on her face or in her body language.

Ansel stepped close and cupped her cheek, an unusually demonstrative gesture. "You are a rare treasure, Gabrielle. I shall miss our evenings."

"As shall I," she returned. *"Ma vie changera."* My life

will change. *"Je crains demain autant que je regrette hier."* I fear tomorrow as much as I regret yesterday.

"Such sweet words of love, my pet," he said with a smile. "I have something for you."

He often brought her perfume or jewelry, but he hadn't arrived with a package in view. Now he slid a hand inside his suit jacket and extricated a slim leather folder. Opening it revealed a ledger. He turned his hand so she could read a deposit report. The balance took her breath away.

"It's a bank account. I considered cash, because it's more prudent, but in the long run, this is secure. Your money is safe, and no one can steal it."

Ella looked from the bankbook to his face. No money had ever been exchanged between them. His paying discreetly kept the veneer of their relationship as lovers in place. Madame Fairchild paid Ella as she did all the other girls, after an allowance for food and clothing was deducted. Granted the gentlemen's fees were exorbitant, but champagne was costly, and Ella's seamstress truly was a Frenchwoman. Ella lived in splendor and ate in elegance, but had very little money to show for four years in the parlor house.

"It's something to fall back on. Something that's all your own and no one else knows about." He closed the ledger and pressed it into her hand. "Understood?"

She nodded. She'd never had more than a few dollars in her entire life. Her mind raced with the coming change and this unexpected windfall.

"That money will take care of you when you need it, so keep this booklet safe."

Ella crushed the folder to her breast, against her wildly beating heart. Tears came to her eyes and she turned her head, blinking to dry them.

"Gabrielle." He took her chin on his curled index finger and raised her head so she was forced to look up at him. "Leave here while you can still make a life for yourself. Right now you're young and beautiful, but a day will come when you're no longer the most desirable girl."

How well she knew. Her mother had barely been forty when she'd died, but she could have passed for Ella's grandmother. Ella had heard talk of women no longer in the blush of youth sent to the bordellos *and worse*. She lived with the fear of a similar fate.

"Do you understand?"

She nodded. *"Je comprends."*

Seeming content that he'd eased his conscience where she was concerned, he moved to stand beside the wooden valet and removed his jacket. "Yes, my pet, I will most certainly miss you."

Mr. Murdock had been gone well over an hour. Ella had bathed and sewn the bankbook into the hem of the velvet traveling coat she'd only worn once. Unable to concentrate on reading, she sat before the cold fireplace, staring into its depths when a timid knock sounded at her door.

She got up and slid back the bolt. "Celeste?"

The petite girl in the well-lit hallway checked behind her. "May I come in?"

Ella opened the door wider and stepped aside. The other girl had never been in Ella's room before, and her eyes widened as she looked around, taking in the elegant furnishings. She didn't remark.

Celeste had already washed her face in preparation for sleep. Closing the door, Ella cringed at the sight of the girl's still-healing lip and nose, which she'd carefully concealed all week. Her straight hair, dyed a coal black because Madame Fairchild believed redheads were a detriment, had been knotted atop her head.

"Are you hurt?" Ella asked. A few slaps or an occasional punch were tolerated, and the servants could have tended to her injuries if that had been the case. Ella couldn't think of any reason why she'd come to her room.

"No, but she let him come back," the girl said. "Just like nothing ever happened. I knew she would."

Ella nodded. She'd known, too.

Celeste reached under her shawl and produced a scrap of newspaper, which she unfolded. "Look at this."

Ella took the crumpled newsprint and read.

Several gentlemen of means in the Wyoming Territory seek young, intelligent, refined maidens of a loving disposition for the purpose of matrimony. Railroad tickets provided upon acceptance by our liaison.

Celeste blinked up at her. "What's a liaison?"

"A contact person."

"I'm done taking punches." Celeste's tone revealed her determination. "I'm getting out of here."

Ella's heart pounded at her words. "You're—you're *leaving?*"

"And I'm never looking back." She studied Ella's expression. "I grew up with a ma and pa, Gabrielle. I had a family once. I went to school and did things like other people, so I know this house is no life for a woman. There's better. I don't care if I have to go hungry on the way to someplace else. I'm getting out of here. All the shrimp cocktails in the world aren't worth a black eye or sore ribs every Friday night. I've already sent a wire in reply."

Ella stared at the clipping until her fingers trembled. For the first time the possibility of leaving became a reality. She desperately wanted to change her situation. With Ansel Murdock gone, her fate now fluttered in the breeze. She could end up like her mother: unloved and alone. The possibility made her feel sick.

She'd been out in public a few times and had learned her skin wasn't thick enough to endure the scorn of the townspeople. It was acceptable for a man to visit a parlor house, but immoral for a woman to work in one.

And now...now she had a bank account just waiting. "Ella," she said.

Celeste frowned. "What?"

"My name is Ella."

Sweetwater, Wyoming, May 1873

Nathan still had reservations about this plan to bring in young women with the intent of matchmaking. The territorial board of directors had strongly suggested he needed a wife to protect his family image if he wanted his name on the ticket to run for governor in the fall. Somehow the talk had evolved into sending for brides, and by no objective of his own, the watchful eyes of his peers and supporters were now upon him.

Leland Howard was the only other man in Sweetwater with a home big enough to entertain a crowd that included the town council members and their wives, all the single businessmen and the newly arrived mail-order brides. Together, the men had decided the Howard place was the best location, being neutral ground and not giving Nathan the advantage of the women seeing his home before they met him.

"That little one's pretty," Tom Bradbury said.

Nathan followed Tom's gaze. The woman he spoke of was tiny with straight jet-black hair and a pinkish complexion. She lifted her hazel-eyed gaze and scanned the crowd, her discomfort momentarily obvious. Too timid for the wife of a governor.

Well, he wasn't governor. In fact, he had yet to see his

name on the ballot; but a wife was a lifetime commitment. He needed one who would be an asset to a campaign and his following terms in office, not to mention a suitable life companion.

As if he was actually thinking about this. He turned to the buffet table and studied the impressive spread. Glancing back at the gathering, a group of men huddling nearly shoulder to shoulder caught his eye. Curiosity got the best of him, and he joined them. Another heated discussion about the demonetizing of silver, no doubt. Those who owned or held shares in mines had debated the bill before President Grant at length.

One of the men noticed Nathan and took a step back in deference to his approach. Another did the same, and an opening formed. Nathan walked right into the center of the gathering. It was there he discovered the most breathtaking creature he'd ever laid eyes on.

Her deep rose-colored dress bared her shoulders, revealing ivory skin as smooth and rich as heavy cream. Her tawny gold hair had been swept into one of those fashionable styles with dangling curls that women seemed to favor. The shiny tresses cascaded over one slender shoulder.

She was replying to something one of the men had asked, when she must have sensed the change in the atmosphere. Her attention flitted from face to face until she spotted him.

Eyes as blue and luminous as a clear mountain lake returned his gaze. High cheekbones and gracefully arched brows gave her a look of sweet sophistication, but her mouth...

Nathan's visceral reaction to the woman surprised him more than anything could have. Her generous lips immediately conjured up sultry images and planted a dozen uncharacteristic fantasies in his head.

He couldn't take a deep breath. This was what it would feel like if someone stood on his chest.

"Nathan," Leland said, urging him forward. "This is Miss Ella Reed from Illinois. Miss Reed, Mr. Lantry."

She offered him her hand. "It's a pleasure, Mr. Lantry."

Her voice was deeper than he'd expected, her diction flawless, her tone sultry without being improper.

She extended her gloved hand, and he took her fingers, touching fabric, but imagining warm soft skin. "The pleasure is entirely mine, Miss Reed." He glanced at the men who'd obviously been monopolizing her attentions. "Have you had a chance to eat?"

"Not yet. I am a bit hungry."

The others took their cue and made their departures. Nathan offered her his arm and led her toward the buffet. "The company of lovely young ladies is uncommon in this part of the country. I'm afraid these men would occupy your entire evening if you let them."

"Everyone's been most kind so far. We've been given splendid rooms at the hotel. The staff is accommodating, and the food is good."

He handed her a plate and located his own.

After selecting a tiny veal tart, she added a few dates to her plate. She stood gazing at a platter of individual chestnut puddings longer than the necessary time it took to select one.

"Is there a problem?" he asked.

"Oh, no," she answered, glancing up sheepishly. "I don't often eat desserts. These look irresistibly good."

She used a flat silver utensil and selected two.

Nathan reached for a fork and handed it to her. "Would you like to sit?"

"I would," she answered with a nod, but she continued to move around the end of the table. Passing the tiny sandwiches, she went directly to the éclairs and used silver tongs to select one. A sugar-encrusted bit of chocolate followed.

He led her out a set of doors to the Howards' garden, lit by burning torches, and gestured to the stone bench.

Miss Reed seated herself and arranged her skirts. He liked the way she carried herself, gracefully, confidently. He liked everything about her: her slender neck and the smooth expanse of skin above the bodice of her dress, where a gold locket winked in the torchlight. Her waist was impossibly narrow.

She took a dainty bite of the pudding and closed her eyes. "Exquisite."

He couldn't help a smile. She held half a plate of sweets. "Are you a cook yourself, Miss Reed?"

Her pleased expression vanished and a concerned frown marred her forehead before she seemed to catch herself and her skin smoothed once again. "Cooking was not one of my studies. But I'm a fast learner and could pick up the skill quickly if need be. Is cooking a requirement of a wife in Sweetwater?"

"I apologize. My question was a bumbling attempt at conversation. I'm sure you could learn to cook. I'd wager most of the men here tonight are unconcerned about cooking skills."

She held her plate in her lap and cast him an interested glance. "Are *you* seeking a wife, Mr. Lantry?"

Chapter Two

~~~~~

He'd gone along with this venture because they did need more women in Sweetwater. He'd listened to the recommendations of the board, but he hadn't committed. He'd had a wife, and he hadn't planned on another. For the past couple of years a woman hadn't been high on his list of priorities. But then...he hadn't met *this* woman. "My fellow board members think a wife would offer a sense of stability and portray a solid family image when I run for an office."

Her clear blue gaze searched his eyes with rapt interest. Their gazes met and held. "Which office would that be?"

He sensed there was more than a confident, beautiful young woman behind the exquisite exterior. "Governor of the territory. Perhaps one day of the state."

"What about you?" she asked. "What do you think?" This time the tone of her voice held a vulnerable edge.

"I have children. A genteel influence would be in their best interest."

"Children?" she asked. "You're a widower?"

"I am."

"My deepest condolences. How many young ones are in your care?"

"Three." This was beginning to sound like an interview, and quite well it should be. He dared guess the tawny-haired miss could have her choice of any man in the house. "Why did a lovely young woman like yourself answer the advertisement and travel West? You don't strike me as an adventuress."

"No, I don't suppose I am. My friend Celeste had already sent a wire, and joining her seemed logical. A fresh start was better than any of the prospects I had at home."

He wouldn't have thought so. "Did you leave behind family?"

"No, my mother—and father—both of my parents, that is, are dead. I have no family."

"That's unfortunate," he said kindly, thinking she was too young to be forced to make life choices alone. But then she carried herself with sophisticated confidence. "You're obviously a city woman. The territory is barely civilized. Our dinner parties and social activities aren't what you're accustomed to."

She glanced down. "You'd be surprised what I'm accustomed to." Taking a breath that beckoned his attention to her breasts beneath the rose-colored material of her dress, she brushed nonexistent crumbs from her skirt. "I'm quite good with figures, so I can keep an account.

I can read music and am accomplished on the piano. I speak French fluently and embroider. And I am well-read. I can tutor students in a variety of subjects, should they require my help."

He still imagined this beautiful, intelligent young woman had her choice of husbands in Illinois. He found it remarkable that she'd left her familiar surroundings and traveled to Wyoming with the intent of marrying. "I'm keeping you from your food, when I meant to rescue you from others doing the same. Please. Enjoy."

She gave him a grateful smile, picked up the éclair and took a dainty bite. "Oh my goodness."

Her enjoyment of the sweet was obvious. After a few minutes, he asked, "Would you care for a cup of tea?"

"That would be nice...but..."

"What?"

"Did I see champagne?"

At her request, he had to deliberately keep his eyebrow from rising on its own. She was a refreshing change from the teetotaler majority of females of his acquaintance. "I'll bring you a glass."

He fetched two glasses, and she accepted one with thanks.

"I've never had the pleasure of satisfying my sweet tooth, so forgive me for appearing a glutton."

"On the contrary," he answered. "You have a dainty appetite." He seated himself beside her. "Éclairs weren't on the menu back home?"

"At Miss Haversham's Academy for Young Women,

we weren't allowed to eat anything that would place our figures at risk."

Now that Nathan thought about it, all of the young women he'd seen so far had been exceedingly trim. "A person deserves a treat now and then," he said with a smile.

She sipped her champagne as though it were an accustomed taste. "Your children," she said. "Girls or boys, and what are their ages?"

"Christopher is my oldest, and he's six. Grace is—"

"There you are, Miss Reed." William Pickering chose that moment to lead a party out of doors. "Nathan is holding our guest captive, I see."

Ella gave Nathan an apologetic look and stood.

"I'll take your plate," he offered.

She handed the dish to Nathan, and an almost pleadingly hopeful look crossed her features before she raised her chin and turned away, joining the others.

William touched her elbow, and something dark and primitive rose inside Nathan. The other man introduced Ella to three young men in the gathering, and the crowd moved back indoors. He was left with an unfamiliar hollowness in his gut. Odd, how she'd affected him so profoundly and left him aching.

"Beautiful evening."

Nathan hadn't realized he'd been staring after the group until the feminine voice spoke from beside him.

"I've never seen so many stars in the heavens," she said. "Never spent much time out of doors looking for them, I guess, but they aren't near as bright in the city."

The woman's dark hair was arranged in an artful upswept twist, with curls that hung on either side of her face. Her pale dress shimmered in the torchlight.

She turned her dark gaze on him. Her smile held a surprising edge of seduction, though he was sure she'd been intending coquettishness. "You're Nathan Lantry?"

"I am." He wanted to follow Ella and make sure the hounds didn't devour her. "And you're...?"

"Lena Kellie."

"Pleasure to meet you."

"Looks as though this town could've used a dozen more women."

"It takes a special breed to flourish here," he replied.

"Think Miss Haversham's girls will do?"

"The men seem to think so."

"What about you?" She met his gaze boldly. "Are you in the market for a bride?"

He hadn't been until half an hour ago. "I might be."

She rested her hand on his coat sleeve and raised her dark eyes up to meet his gaze. "Seen anything you like yet?"

Her overture didn't rest easy with him. He'd seen someone he liked a lot. "Would you care for a glass of champagne?"

"Thank you, yes."

"Join me inside," he suggested and led her toward the house.

* * *

Ella's last full breath had been drawn an hour ago in the garden. Since then she'd been gawked at, showered with smiles, spoken of when men didn't think she was paying attention and fed enough éclairs to burst the seams of her evening dress. Once the gentlemen discovered her fondness for desserts, each successive guest had come bearing a sweet.

How long was this civilized cattle auction going to last? Two men had proposed upon introduction. Three others had requested her hand in marriage after a few pleasantries. She'd never imagined it would be this easy to find a husband. But how on earth would she choose?

She looked them over now. The youngest one with the shy smile and the sandy-colored sideburns seemed the safest and the most endearing. He was rather boyish actually, and youth and innocence had its charm. The oldest gentleman appeared the wealthiest however, and his asset was definitely one worthy of consideration. Age made no difference as long as a husband was a good man. But this one had a tick that inched his cheek up into a squint every few minutes. No matter how rich he was, that trait might get distracting over dinner for the next thirty or forty years.

Celeste seemed taken with a tall fellow Ella had learned was a rancher. He had kind eyes and a warm smile, but she knew well that looks could be deceiving. It was imperative that Celeste find someone kind. Ella wished she could be certain of his character.

The conversation swelled into a buzz around her. The room had grown uncomfortably warm. She studied the circle of men for an opening and spotted Nathan Lantry. He stood like a solid beacon in a rolling sea. Though all of the men were dressed similarly, Nathan wore his dark suit and white shirt with an elegant style that drew attention to his height and the breadth of his shoulders.

His cheekbones were sharp and his brows dark slashes, but his kind eyes and well-shaped lips softened his appearance.

"Excuse me," she said to the nearest suitor and worked her way toward Nathan. Lena stood beside him. Spotting Ella, a predatory gleam lit her features. She took a step closer to Nathan and gave Ella a glare.

"Is everything all right?" Ella asked her in a quiet voice.

"Everything is just fine," Lena replied, but looked away.

"I need to ask Mr. Lantry a question." Ella turned to the man. "I wonder if I might have a word with you."

"Certainly." He glanced at Lena. "Excuse us." He led Ella out to a wide wood-paneled hallway, lined with oversize oil paintings of various landscapes and hunting scenes. Small tables were draped with fringed scarves and held candlesticks and bric-a-brac. "What is it, Miss Reed?"

"The rancher named Adams. Do you know him?"

"Paul Adams? Yes, I know him. Are you thinking of marrying Adams?"

"No, my friend Celeste is thinking of accepting his

proposal." Was that a look of relief that crossed his elegant features? "But I want to be certain he's a trustworthy sort. Not given to violence."

He raised his eyebrows in surprise, but answered immediately. "Paul's a good fellow. Honest and hardworking. Treats his hands well from what I know. Just built a house on the southwest portion of his land last summer. Not far from town."

"Would he be a considerate spouse, do you reason?"

Their gazes met and held longer than it took him to form a reply. Ella recognized when a man was attracted to her, but for the first time she experienced a positive reaction to his interest. She felt unexplainably safe with him.

"I don't have any grounds to think otherwise." He glanced aside and then back at her.

"Thank you."

Nathan Lantry's discomfort was obvious. He didn't know anything about her, so the irritating prickle of shame she experienced wasn't because of his censure. She must have been mistaken about the interest she thought she'd glimpsed. She turned back toward the doorway.

Nathan shouldn't have been disappointed that she'd only wanted to ask a question on behalf of a friend. What had he anticipated?

Besides her beauty, Ella Reed was cultured, well mannered and graceful. Her concern for her friend's wellbeing touched him. He'd be a fool not to recognize her as a perfect partner for a man in his position. Besides her obvious external qualifications, she had a compassionate nature and could provide a gentle influence for his children.

"What about you?" he asked before she could slip from the hallway.

She turned back. "What about me?"

"Have you singled someone out? Want to ask me about a prospect for yourself?"

She took a few steps back toward him without reply.

"Has anyone asked you?" he asked.

She nodded.

"Who?"

"The newspaperman."

"Lewis Frost."

She nodded. "The rancher from South Pass. He has a spread overlooking a valley."

Nathan had a difficult time picturing her on a ranch.

She thought a moment. "Mr. Pickering."

Three of them? William Pickering wasn't a bad sort, but he did spend Friday and Saturday nights in the saloon.

"And a handful of others."

Six altogether? Eight? Of course he wasn't surprised. Every man in the gathering would recognize her as a suitable prospect as easily as he had. A prize like her didn't come along every day. Not even once a lifetime, he'd wager.

However, the last thing he wanted to do was rush into

a second marriage and risk another woman's dissatisfaction. His wife hadn't known what she was getting into by marrying him and coming West. She'd done her best, but their courtship had been rushed—she wouldn't have married him if she'd known all that was involved—and she'd never really been happy.

But Ella Reed had come West on her own. She planned to marry one of the men who'd proposed tonight. He wasn't sure how she'd fare with one of the others, but *he* would treat her the way a lady deserved. She would do well marrying him. She could learn to love his children and they her. His heart hammered. With impulsiveness he'd regret later, he groped for the correct words. "I'd be honored if you'd add me to your list of prospects, Miss Reed."

Her blue gaze flickered in the light from the nearby gas lamp on the wall.

The sensation in his belly felt as though he'd leaped off a cliff. Perhaps he had.

"*You,* Mr. Lantry?"

"I'm asking for your hand in marriage. I'd make a good husband. I have help for the children and someone who cooks, so I'm not asking because I need you to perform household chores."

She listened without a visible reaction.

"I'm asking because I believe we could develop a mutually satisfying relationship."

Her gaze didn't waver from his. "I understand."

Had he said enough to convince her he was the best choice? "I'm the city attorney. I own three lucrative businesses in town. My children and I attend Mount Calvary Church on a regular basis. I'm on the town council board, and I don't—"

"I accept."

Chapter Two

Chapter Three

He blinked, gathering his wits, undoubtedly looking like a fool. "Just like that?"

"It's not a difficult decision."

Should he be flattered?

Nathan released a breath. He was relieved. More relieved than the situation deemed logical. He'd never met Ella Reed until this evening. His heart wouldn't have been broken if she'd chosen Lewis Frost or William Pickering. But he knew instinctively that he'd have regretted letting the moment pass without giving a proposal his best effort. "I give you my word I won't disappoint you."

She smiled, but the expression didn't reach her eyes, which still held an edge of concern. But her words belied worry. "I don't doubt that."

"The city is paying for the hotel rooms throughout the end of the week," he told her. "If you need a little time to plan a wedding or—or to acclimate yourself, I'll arrange to keep your room."

"I only know four people to invite to a wedding, and I wouldn't know the first thing about planning one. I can figure it out if you like. But not for my sake, please. A small ceremony will suffice."

"I'll make arrangements then," he offered. "I expect the minister will be busy after tonight."

Ella had no schoolgirl fantasies about a fancy church wedding or a white satin dress. Marrying Nathan Lantry was the best and most secure move she would ever make to seal her future. She would have stood on a wooden crate in a Kansas dust storm to say her vows.

Footsteps sounded and Lena appeared through the doorway opening. Her intent gaze zeroed in on Nathan, and she made a beeline toward him. "There you are. I missed your company."

Nathan glanced at Ella. "Shall we make our announcement now?"

She nodded in agreement.

"Announcement?" Lena frowned at Ella.

"I've accepted Mr. Lantry's proposal," Ella whispered.

The other woman's frown turned into a scowl. "I might've known."

She gathered her skirts and swished away into the main room.

Nathan touched the small of Ella's back and guided her to a prominent place in the noisy gathering. The innocent touch seemed at once proprietary and comforting.

He unerringly found Leland Murdock and leaned to say something to the man in private. Leland's eyebrows shot up. He gave Ella a broad smile, then turned to the crowd. "May I have your attention, please!"

The cacophony of voices fell to a murmur and then expectant silence.

"We have our first announcement," Leland called.

Murmurs tittered through the bystanders.

Leland gave Nathan a nod.

Nathan stepped forward. "I guess I'll be the first," he said. He glanced from one face to another. "I've asked Miss Ella Reed to be my wife." The room fell perfectly silent. "She's accepted."

A cheer rose, followed by a few grumbles, which had been expected. Celeste darted around a couple of men to reach Ella. She threw her arms around her. "I'm so happy for you."

The lanky rancher Nathan had called Paul Adams pushed past a few people to stand in the space that had opened. "I have another announcement."

"Go ahead, Paul," Leland prompted.

Color rose in Paul's face, but he drew a breath to say, "I'm marryin' Celeste, here."

He turned to look for Celeste, and she joined him by taking his hand and smiling ear to ear.

By the time another hour had passed, four of the women were pledged to local men. Nearly everyone had made a match. Everyone except Lena. Certainly her lack of commitment wasn't for lack of proposals. Lena was undoubtedly holding out for a better offer.

Ella, on the other hand, would never get a better opportunity than the one she had right now.

Ella's bridegroom had arranged a ceremony for Saturday afternoon. Two other couples planned to marry that same day, both scheduled in the morning. Ella attended both ceremonies, one in the judge's chambers in a small building beside the sheriff's office and the other at the Methodist church. After a joint informal reception, she hurried back to the hotel to prepare for her own wedding.

Though Celeste had been married only a few hours, she and her new husband remained in town for Ella's wedding, which would take place at Nathan's church. Ella couldn't have been more relieved to hear her knock and opened the door to admit her.

"Did you ever think it?" Celeste asked. "Did you ever in your wildest imaginings think we'd be brides?"

Ella shook her head. "Or that we'd be married to upstanding citizens and able to walk about town without scorn. I was greeted politely half a dozen times on my way to your ceremony this morning."

"We got wedding gifts." Elation buoyed Celeste's tone. She buttoned the remaining buttons on the back of Ella's pale peach dress and fastened a string of pearls around her neck. "Quilts and dishes and such. Paul has family nearby. Did you see all of them in the judge's chambers?"

Ella turned to face her, hoping for all she was worth that Paul Adams was every bit the man of character

Nathan had assured her he was. "You will come to me if he's...unkind, won't you? I have some money, and I can pay for a hotel or train fare."

Celeste nodded. "Don't worry. Paul's a good man, Ella." Her smile faltered. "We're all doing what we had to do, but we might as well make the most of it. Once tonight has passed, I'll be able to handle everything else."

Ella gave her a questioning look. "What do you mean?"

"We're supposed to be innocent virgins the first time."

"Oh, yes," Ella agreed. She'd thought of the coming night, as well, but she hadn't let herself dwell on it.

"Just cry a little," Celeste suggested. "And don't appear eager. We're good girls now."

"I'll remember," Ella replied with a nod.

"Why do you suppose Lena is holding out?" Celeste asked, changing the subject.

"She wasn't happy about Nathan asking me to marry him," Ella replied. "That was obvious."

"Your man is one of the richest in the territory," Celeste agreed. "That probably stuck in her craw."

Ella liked the sound of Nathan referred to as *her man*.

"Since Lena couldn't have him, she probably wants the next-wealthiest man for herself. I'm just glad I got a kind one. I'm not going to mind cooking or cleaning or even helping with ranch work, as long as Paul is mild tempered."

Ella checked her timepiece and ushered Celeste toward the door. Paul waited in the hotel foyer, his hat in his hands.

"Mr. Lantry sent a carriage for you," he said and gestured toward the door. "And he's even invited us to the reception."

Sure enough a black carriage pulled by two fine horses with shiny mahogany coats waited in the street. "There's room for the three of us," Ella offered.

All three weddings she'd ever attended had been on this same day, and all three were ceremonies she'd never imagined to attend, especially not her own. Butterflies created havoc in Ella's stomach as the three of them traveled across town. She composed her nerves before Paul helped her step down from the carriage and led both women to the door.

Inside, the late-afternoon sun streamed through stained glass windows, illuminating depictions of Christ in various settings. A garden scene extended its long green shadows as far as Nathan's feet, where he stood at the front of the middle aisle.

Three fair-haired children in their Sunday finest stood in stair-step alignment and craned their necks to watch Ella's approach. She gave each a hesitant smile. Her stomach quivered and her head felt light. This was the best day of her life, but she didn't know the least thing about children...or about being a wife.

Dressed elegantly in pinstripe black pants, Nathan wore a black jacket over a crisp white shirt with a white bow tie. Seeing him dressed so formally brought the reality of this moment into sharp focus. She was pledging herself to this startlingly handsome man, who was but a stranger.

And he in turn was binding himself—and his young family—to her, a woman he knew nothing about, and yet he accepted her.

She was going to do her very best to live up to his expectations and his trust. Whatever it took to endear her to him and make their marriage work, she vowed to throw herself into wholeheartedly. This act saved her from a lifetime of servitude and a bleak future. He would never regret making her his wife.

Ella was going to make Nathan Lantry a happy man.

Her first glimpse of her new home took Ella's breath away. In the semidarkness, the stately three-story brick house nestled between towering oaks on a parklike lawn. Directly to one side and behind was a carriage house with glowing lanterns on both front corners.

Nathan helped Ella and the children down, and a weathered fellow came to take the buggy and horses.

Squares of light spilled from the first floor windows of the house. Several other carriages and wagons had preceded them, the occupants apparently inside.

The woman Nathan had introduced as Virginia Shippen took little Robby's hand as they approached the house. The short good-natured woman was at least twenty years older than Ella, with a ready smile and an ample waist and hips. The three-year-old kept looking up at Ella with questioning blue eyes, then quickly looking away when she smiled at him.

Grace, the four-year-old, observed Ella with silent curiosity. During the buggy ride, she had directed her attention to her tiny reticule. She wore her sandy hair in two long braids that bounced against the frilly sleeves of her dress when she ran toward the front door.

Nathan's oldest child, Christopher, wore a solemn expression, but walked ahead to be the first to open the door and usher Ella inside. "This is our house," he told her importantly.

His hair was darker than the other two children's and parted with severe precision. Once inside, he gazed up at her, revealing hazel eyes fringed with long black lashes.

"Thank you, Christopher."

His cheeks pinkened, and he glanced away.

A woman in a black dress and white apron met them to take hats and wraps. Ella wore only a scrap of Venetian lace on a pearl comb, which she left in her hair.

They had entered into a foyer lit by a gas chandelier. Voices and music spilled from the open room to the right.

"Papa, are we allowed to stay up for the party?" Christopher asked.

"Of course," Nathan replied. "This is a special night. You may have an hour to greet our guests and eat. After that Mrs. Shippen will see you off to bed, and I'll tuck you in."

Christopher's grin lit his face and revealed charming dimples in each cheek.

Robby extended both arms to Nathan, and the man picked him up. "I imagine you're a little confused about today, aren't you?"

The child nestled his head on Nathan's shoulder. Nathan patted his back through the miniature suit jacket and laid his head against the boy's while Ella watched their interaction with interest.

She'd never seen a man interact with his children before. Observing their little family filled her with a sad yearning. Ella had never known a father's love or attention. She doubted her mother even knew who her father had been, and if she had, the man wouldn't have acknowledged her. These children were privileged in more ways than financially. They had a loving father, a man who willingly played a role in their lives and was concerned for them.

She'd become a recipient of his care and attention, as well. She'd never welcomed change as much as she did now. A shiver of expectation gripped her.

"Are you all right?" Nathan caught her attention.

"Yes. Perfectly."

"Then let's go greet our guests, shall we?"

Besides Nathan's tender concern for his children, Ella had so much to take in all at once: the size of Nathan's home and the lovely furnishings; the guests, dressed in elegant clothing, who milled about and stopped to wish them well; the way his peers looked up to him and honored him by attending his wedding and reception.

All but one of the other girls with whom Ella had come West were in attendance. Instinctively Ella knew that regardless of their new husbands' positions—or lack thereof—in the community, they'd been invited and accepted as Ella's friends.

"Thank you for including Celeste and the others in the reception," she said during a brief moment alone with Nathan.

He had handed her a glass of champagne and, after she had sipped the bubbly liquid, smiled. His warm awareness brought a surprising heat to her cheeks. "Of course your friends are welcome," he said.

Why his attention embarrassed her, she couldn't fathom. She hadn't blushed in years, and all he'd done was smile at her. "I—I haven't seen Lena."

"I sent an invitation that included a guest," he said. "She declined. I'm sorry she slighted you."

Ella shrugged. "We aren't close friends."

"Your friend Celeste will be less than an hour's ride from Sweetwater," he told her. "If you should want to call on her, I'll make arrangements whenever it pleases you. I'm sure being in a new place will be an adjustment for both of you."

"That's kind of you," she said in surprise.

He glanced away as though thinking, but brought his gaze back to hers. "I want you to be happy."

The intimate low timbre of his voice, the words spoken softly for her alone, hammered a dent in her self-protective layer of aloof dignity.

The warmth that had been in her cheeks now spread

to her chest and squeezed her heart until it ached. No one had ever said that to her. No one had ever cared about her happiness. She didn't know how to react—or how to believe him. But she wanted to, and she wanted to revel in the luxury.

Even if words had come to her, she couldn't have spoken them. For the first time, she wondered about his previous wife, the woman he'd loved. If he was this kind to her—a woman he'd only met, how must it have been to be loved by such a man?

What did a love like that feel like?

Immediately, Ella caught herself giving way to fanciful thoughts and reined them in. She'd come to Sweetwater with the intent of gaining respectability and finding a safe haven. She wasn't hitching her wagon to a star. Being Nathan's wife and gaining his respect as well as that of the community was all she'd hoped for. Above everything now she wanted to be worthy of him and deserving of his trust.

A couple joined them then, and Nathan introduced her to Eldon and Rowena Templeton.

"I understand you're from Illinois," Eldon said. "What's the land like in that part of the country?"

"It's green, with lush fields of beans and winding rivers," she replied as though she actually knew first-hand. She'd heard about the Illinois landscape from a man back at Madame Fairchild's dinner table. All she knew firsthand were flat prairies and dry Kansas dust kicked up by endless herds of cattle led from the trail to the stockyard pens—and even those scenes she'd taken in through closed and barred windows.

"It sounds lovely," his wife said. "I know Nathan is glad you chose to travel to Wyoming, but it must be quite a change for you."

"It's a big change," she answered. "And all for the better."

Rowena gave Nathan a grin. "You are a lucky man, Nathan Lantry."

"Yes, ma'am," he agreed.

He gazed down at Ella, and she gave him the smile his friends expected. He wrapped his arm around her waist, and she leaned against him. They stood hip to hip, more or less, and she was the first to break their locked gaze and look away.

With all the attention and after meeting so many new people, she'd grown tired, but she kept her fatigue and emotions well disguised. When the guests at last took their leave a few at a time, Nathan assured her it was acceptable for her to excuse herself and go upstairs. "The last room on the right," he told her. "I'm afraid your things aren't unpacked, but you'll have plenty of time to settle in over the next few days."

Climbing the stairs, she left the murmur of voices below to find the room he'd indicated. Oil lamps lit the generous space in a welcoming glow, and she wondered who had made the preparations. The woman in the black dress and white apron who'd answered the door perhaps?

Her six enormous trunks were neatly lined against

one wall, and she opened each to find her hairbrushes, nightgowns and toiletries.

A pitcher of water and towels had been placed on a stand behind a divider brightly painted with peacocks and oriental flowers. Ella was well practiced at unbuttoning the low-cut back of her gown, and she quickly stepped from her dress and hung it over the screen before stripping out of her underclothing. She washed with the thick cloth and her fragrant soap and then dried.

After using glycerin on her elbows, hands and feet, she dusted her body with talc and pulled a shimmery sheer gown over her head. She took time to brush out her hair and sparingly rouge her lips and cheeks. She unwrapped jewelry that had been rolled in stockings, placed the stockings in a drawer and the necklaces and rings back in a wooden chest. She poked through the gemstones, each of them reminding her of the life she wanted to forget. Without selecting an item, she closed the box and tucked it into the bottom drawer of the bureau. Lastly, she slipped on a silk dressing gown and belted the sash at her waist.

Ella dabbed perfume behind her knees and a little on her décolletage and examined her reflection in the mirror. Everything about her new life was unfamiliar... everything but this. The one thing she knew how to do was please Nathan when he came to their room.

Chapter Four

The thought of pleasing her new husband had her looking around the room one more time. She opened the closet to find bare pegs and the shelves barren save for extra blankets. The bureau drawers held nothing but the items she'd placed in them. There was no sign of the man or his belongings.

He owned an enormous well-furnished house with many bedrooms. Apparently she had her own. Was that usual? She had no inkling of normal sleeping arrangements for husbands and wives.

She put away the rest of her lingerie and hung several dresses to pass the time, but she was tired and eventually perched on the chair before the cold fireplace and studied a still life of fruit spilling from a basket. The painting hung by a gold cord from the crown molding over the mantel.

Her eyelids were drooping when after several minutes a knock sounded at the door.

Ella crossed the room to open it.

Nathan stood in the hallway, his broad form and dark hair lit by the wall lamps, still dressed in the formal clothing he'd worn for the ceremony and reception. With a welcoming smile, she stepped back to allow him to enter.

His gaze fell immediately to her dressing gown, and the lace that peeked from the deep V where the front overlapped. He swallowed.

Break the ice. "It was a lovely party, Nathan. Thank you."

He drew his attention to her face. "It was my pleasure."

Make him welcome. "I was waiting for you."

Stepping in, he closed the door, but didn't turn the key in the lock. Once he stepped farther into the room, she took the initiative and locked the door.

His slight frown revealed uncertainty. "I'd like to talk to you."

"I'm eager to hear what you have to say. Would you like to sit? Let me help you remove your jacket."

He kept his gaze from wavering to the bed. "Please. Have a seat."

He waited until she had settled on the settee and then took a chair across from her. "I'm aware that our marriage is unconventional," he began.

She had no experience with marriage, conventional or otherwise. "I intend to be a good wife, Nathan."

"I appreciate that," he replied. "And more than

anything I hope you'll be comfortable and content here. Everything is new to you. The territory. This marriage. Because of the circumstances, we were forced to make decisions quickly, and that's not an ideal condition. Courting gives a couple time to learn about each other, time to grow comfortable and at ease."

"I don't feel cheated," she said. "I'm prepared to be your wife."

"Ella," he said kindly, "there are aspects to marriage that shouldn't be rushed. You're young, with tender sensibilities, and I refuse to take advantage of you by consummating our marriage while you're unprepared."

At last his hesitancy took shape in her mind. "You don't intend to come to my bed tonight."

"No."

"Will you be sleeping in another room?"

"I've given you your own room for privacy's sake."

A sinking sensation settled in her chest, dangerously close to her heart. He didn't want her? Ella kept her features passive and calm, but inside she quaked with uncertainty. Fear got a tiny foothold on her confidence. What had she gotten herself into? Half a dozen men had looked at her with lusty thoughts swimming in their gleaming eyes, and she had chosen to marry the one man who didn't desire her?

How would she prove herself—endear herself to him? How would their relationship be sealed?

"I intend to court you, Ella. You deserve enough time to come to terms with a marriage and all it entails.

We will observe a courtship period before we become intimate."

She remembered to breathe. "And how long would that be?"

"I have my mind set on six months."

Six months? Why entire towns sprang up in less time. Wars were fought and… "What will we do for six months?"

"We'll get to know each other."

Her thoughts traveled back to his proposal. *I'm not asking because I need you to perform household chores,* he'd said. *I'm asking because I believe we could develop a mutually satisfying relationship.*

At the time she'd known exactly what that meant. She still understood. He hadn't needed her to clean or cook or even to look after his children. She would have learned how, but all those tasks were taken care of. No, he wanted her because he needed a woman at his side in public and in his bed in private. *Hadn't he?*

But because he believed she'd come from a genteel background and was like any other young unmarried woman her age, he believed she needed protection and shelter…a slow tender initiation to the ways between men and women.

She appreciated him all the more for his concern. But she was all the more determined to win his favor. "Will you kiss me?"

"I—" He had obvious trouble forming his reply.

"Is kissing part of courtship?" she insisted.

"Yes. Most certainly it is."

She rose to her feet. "Then I'd like you to kiss me."

When he stood and stepped forward, she tipped her head back to look up at him. Still, he hadn't closed all the distance between them. She took the step that brought her against him and rested her hand on the front of his jacket. Parting her lips, she waited.

Instead of bending forward and covering her mouth with his as she expected, he raised his hand to her cheek and cupped it. With grave tenderness, he slid his fingertips into the hair at her nape. An unanticipated shiver ran across her shoulder and down to her breasts, tightening them beneath the silk wrapper.

He rested his other hand ever-so-lightly against the small of her back, riveting her in place with that gentle touch.

His dark gaze traveled her face, from her eyes to her lips, his expression changing...relaxing. Yes. He wanted her. Relief swept over her. "You are a rare flower, Ella. An exquisite rare flower."

His breath touched her chin. Her heart leaped in response.

She truly wanted him to kiss her. She no longer had a point to prove or an agenda. Ella wanted this man to kiss her. Unfamiliar tears smarted behind her eyelids, so she closed her eyes to hide them.

He raised her face with his palm, and his lips closed over hers in a warm tantalizing greeting. *Hello. So this is what you taste like.*

She wrapped her arm behind his neck and urged him closer, into a fuller, more satisfying melding of lips and breath. He smelled good, like crisp linen with a hint of mint and champagne. His lips were firm and warm. Her head felt as though she'd finished a bottle on her own, but she'd only had two glasses of the bubbly liquid. The man himself was intoxicating.

She'd had no idea there were kisses like this. She kissed him because she wanted to, because the act gave her pleasure. The recognition shocked her.

Maybe courtship wasn't going to be so bad, after all.

He drew back a few inches. She opened her eyes and he gazed into them. Was he changing his mind? Would this champagne kiss lead to a night in her bed?

"I'd better leave," he said.

She'd never quite understood disappointment in this heartfelt *physical* manner. She wasn't a dreamer. Dreams were out of reach and easily destroyed. Nor was she a romantic, holding hopeless imaginings of love or faithfulness. She knew firsthand the true nature of men. She held no expectations, therefore experienced no disenchantment. His leaving was a mere frustration, she assured herself. She had a plan to endear herself to him, and he had thwarted that with his counterplan for a courtship.

Ella released her hold on his neck and took a backward step on legs that trembled. His hooded gaze took in her hair, her lips, and fell to the base of her throat, where she suspected her pulse beat wildly. She gave him a demure smile.

He would change his mind within a week.

* * *

She'd been alone her whole life, so the solitude of her room was nothing new. The most unusual aspect she discovered was upon waking when she drew back the russet damask draperies to greet the morning. She had a clear view of the immense side yard, the roof of the carriage house and the broad expanse of sky—all without bars.

The females who lived there had been told that the iron bars that covered every window at Madame Fairchild's were for their own protection. Men in a cow town would do just about anything to get to a woman. But more often those barriers had prevented the girls from taking a notion to leave.

Ella studied the neighboring house with its painted gables and glanced at the roofs of the other nearby homes. Yesterday one of the men had mentioned that vast improvements had been made to the streets and buildings along the main thoroughfares in hopes of having a governor chosen from Sweetwater. The locals had expectations of a territorial capitol and eventually statehood. She raised the window to the sound of a horse and buggy clattering on the brick street.

Sights and sounds of freedom.

For the first time, she recognized what marriage to Nathan Lantry had bought her. Freedom to come and go as she pleased, freedom to walk along the street and to shop with her head held high. Freedom to enjoy life without oppression or criticism.

Ella wanted to become the person Nathan believed

he'd married. And she would. Now that she had the opportunity, she could blend herself into this community and become his most valuable asset.

She washed quickly, arranged her hair and donned a pastel green day dress. She was thankful that her wardrobe had been designed and created by the talented seamstress Madame Fairchild kept on her staff. The Frenchwoman traveled abroad at least once a year to update her fashion knowledge and buy fabrics and notions.

Without anyone ever saying as much, Ella understood she'd be expected to live up to the caliber of dress and conduct befitting a governor's wife. She donned a strand of pearls and a jade brooch appropriate for day wear.

The upstairs hall was quiet, but sounds of activity rose from downstairs. In the dining room, she discovered Nathan and the children seated at one end of a massive table.

He stood and held a chair out for her. "Did you sleep well?"

"I did, thank you."

The children observed her in silence. "Good morning," she said. She noticed an extra place setting and wondered who would be joining them.

Mrs. Shippen arrived through a doorway with a pitcher of milk she poured into the children's glasses. She seated herself in front of the other place setting.

Footsteps sounded and a plump woman entered from the kitchen, carrying a steaming platter of sliced ham and a plate of fried eggs. She handed the platter to Nathan and set the plate within his reach.

"Ella, this is Charlotte Miller." He served Christopher and himself and passed both dishes to Ella. "Charlotte, my new wife."

"How do, Mizz Lantry," the woman said with a friendly smile.

"It's a pleasure, Mrs. Miller."

"Just Charlotte," the woman said.

Ella took servings from each plate and passed the dishes to Mrs. Shippen, who served the other two children and proceeded to cut their ham into bite-size pieces.

"Charlotte's a fine cook," Nathan assured her. "She's here every morning, and each night. After breakfast on Sunday, she leaves a noon meal in the oven."

Robby slumped in his chair and pouted.

"What's the matter, Robby?" his father asked.

"I want applesauce."

Nathan glanced at the cook. "Do we have applesauce?"

The woman nodded.

Ella folded her hands in her lap and didn't lift her gaze to watch the exchange. She'd never sat at a table with a family in her life. If Nathan was mustering up a load of steam to reprimand the child, she didn't want to be a witness. In her experience children ate what was placed in front of them without options or complaints.

Nathan stood, resting his napkin on his seat. "I'll be right back."

Ella's heart rate increased a measure in her discomfort.

Robby remained slumped on the chair, swinging his feet under the table.

Mrs. Shippen unconcernedly served herself eggs and picked up her fork.

Nathan returned and Robby sat up straight with a bright smile. "You will eat an egg, too," Nathan told him, spooning thick applesauce onto his plate.

Nodding happily, the boy picked up his spoon and ate.

Nathan returned to his seat and glanced at Ella's plate. "Something wrong with the food?"

"Not at all." Ella relaxed and smeared a spoonful of preserves on a slice of toast.

"No jam at Miss Haversham's, either?" he asked.

"No jam," she replied. "Dry toast and tea."

"Doesn't sound like a meal for growing children."

She took her first bite to discover a pleasant burst of sweet raspberry flavor. Nothing about her life had been ordinary, but she had no idea what ordinary involved. "Is this a normal breakfast for you?" she asked. "Or is this a special occasion?"

"Your first day with us is a special occasion, but this is a typical breakfast. When Charlotte needs a day off, we make the best of it. Mrs. Shippen isn't a bad cook."

Virginia Shippen spoke up for the first time, directing her remark to Ella. "The mister can stir up a fine kettle of cooked oats."

"Mrs. Shippen has asked for a day off each week now that you're here," Nathan said.

"May I watch after the children that day?" Ella asked.

Nathan smiled. "I hoped you would."

"I'm happy to do all I can," she said. "And I'll help clean up after breakfast," Ella offered.

"I doubt you'll have time today," Mrs. Shippen told her.

"Why not?"

"You've forgotten," Nathan said. "It's Sunday. Mrs. Shippen's son comes to get her for the day, and Charlotte will clean up. We head out for church in—" he withdrew his pocket watch and flipped open the cover "—about twenty-five minutes."

"Yes, of course." Ella absorbed that piece of information with a calm smile pasted on her face. Of course it was Sunday, and everyone was up early and dressed for church. She glanced at Grace in her green plaid dress and the boys in white shirts and miniature ties. "Am I dressed appropriately?"

Nathan's attention flickered over her hair and touched on her dress. His gaze warmed in appreciation. "You look lovely."

She gripped her napkin in her lap. She had evening dresses aplenty, a selection of day dresses and a few skirts with blouses, but she'd never had occasion to own clothing for church. "I wasn't sure what the ladies in Sweetwater wore to church, is all. I don't want to make a bad impression. Perhaps I should wear a dress with a jacket."

"You'd be too warm," he replied. "I like what you're wearing."

"I'll just go select a hat then." She stood.

"You've barely eaten anything," he said.

"It was very good, but I'm full. I'll be down in time to leave." She hurried from the room and up the stairs, where she dragged a stack of hatboxes to the center of the room and tossed off the lids. Finally deciding, she donned a black straw hat with a small brim. Tiny yellow and red silk flowers adorned the brim, and ends of frothy black netting hung down her back. Standing before the mirror, she settled it just right and stuck a long pearl-headed pin through each side, catching her hair.

She lifted the tray from a trunk and rifled the contents until she found a pair of short white gloves with bead and seed pearl design. This was her debut morning as Mrs. Nathan Lantry. Nerves jittered in her stomach, chipping away at her always-firm composure. These new circumstances were out of her realm of confidence, but she couldn't let her serene facade slip.

The hat didn't go well with her dress, so she removed her hat and tugged off the gloves, then changed into a white handkerchief blouse and donned a short-sleeved plum-colored velvet jacket. The color required she select a different hat, so she barely made it down the stairs and out the door as Nathan was helping the children into a buggy.

"You look lovely," he told her, and held her arm as she climbed in.

"I noticed the carriage house from the window, but where are the horses kept?" she asked.

"I stable two horses at the livery. The liveryman or one of his helpers brings one to the house on Sunday mornings. Whenever you want to go somewhere and don't want to walk, simply let me know in the morning, and I'll make arrangements for a driver to come hitch up the buggy."

She would want to go visit Celeste soon, but for now all she could focus on was this morning.

This was her only chance for a first impression. She hoped for all she was worth that she measured up to the standards of the townspeople...and that Nathan would have no reason to be embarrassed by his hasty choice in a wife.

Chapter Five

The oak doors were already closed, so Nathan tugged one open. Organ music swelled as he gestured for Ella to enter ahead of him. She stepped into the white frame church, her boot heels echoing on the floorboards as she hesitated at the rear of the long aisle. Everyone had been seated, and now heads turned as Nathan guided her forward, the children in tow. Discomfort prickled at the collar of Ella's modest white blouse, and she tried to walk more quietly. Beside and behind her the children's feet made a clatter.

The only familiar face in an ocean of strangers was Celeste's. Ella latched on to her smile and returned it. Was Nathan ever going to select a pew and get them out of the center of attention?

He led them almost all the way to the front before stepping aside and gesturing for her to enter and take a seat on a long pew. Settling beside her, Nathan set down a leather book with a worn cover and pulled Robby onto his lap. He withdrew a small leather case from his pocket and handed it to the boy.

With chubby fingers, the child popped open the snap and slid out a pair of miniature wooden sheep and a giraffe.

Reverend Kane, who had married them the day before, announced a song and page number. Everyone stood. Ella glanced around and followed Nathan's movements. He got to his feet holding Robby on one arm. Nathan gestured toward the back of the pew ahead of them.

It took her a moment to figure out he wanted her to pick up the book that was tucked in a holder. She did so and, following the actions of the person on the other side of her, opened it to the appropriate page.

She read music, so she had no difficulty following along as Reverend Kane led the hymn. Singing in a group of people was outside her experience. Voices lifted all around her, a woman behind them even providing pleasant harmony. Nathan had a surprisingly deep mellow voice, and didn't appear the least self-conscious; in fact, he looked over at her and smiled more than once as they stood like that, voices and organ music swelling around them.

Brass plates were passed from person to person, and Ella observed the church members tossing in coins and paper currency. She leaned toward Nathan to whisper, "I forgot my coin purse."

"No worries. I make our offering for the family. You can put it in the offering plate if you like." He reached into his inside coat pocket, withdrew several bills and handed them to her. She added them to the growing pile of cash as the plate came past.

Reverend Kane stood behind a wooden pulpit draped with a white cloth. "It's my pleasure to make introductions this morning," he said in his booming voice. "Mrs. Paul Adams is with us for the first time. Welcome to Sweetwater, Mrs. Adams."

All heads, including Ella's, turned toward Celeste. Her cheeks burned a bright pink, but she smiled and acknowledged the introduction with a nod. Beside her, Paul beamed with pride.

"And Mrs. Nathan Lantry is worshipping with us for the first time. Welcome to Sweetwater, Mrs. Lantry."

This time men, women and children turned their attention to Ella. Warmth climbed her neck until her cheeks burned hot. She made a point of looking at Celeste and smiling.

The preacher opened a book, and Ella missed his next few words.

"Can you reach my Bible?" Nathan asked, around Robby's head.

Ella must have given him a quizzical look.

"It's there on the other side of you now."

"Oh." She found the book he wanted and extended it toward him.

"Go ahead and hold it for me," he whispered.

She placed it on her lap.

"Open with me to the second book of Corinthians," Reverend Kent instructed.

Pages rustles in the silence as people all around opened their Bibles.

Ella opened the book on her lap, only to see a page header that read Ezekiel thirty-five. She peeked at the book the woman on her left held, and noted she had found the Corinthians heading. After thumbing through a few pages, she realized she was the only one still rustling pages, without seeing anything close to a Corinthian. She quickly closed Nathan's Bible.

His fingers closed over it and he shifted Robby in order to open the book to the correct place.

Toward the end of the service, Robby became irritable, and Nathan kept him quiet by galloping the giraffe across the little boy's knees until he giggled and Nathan had to stop.

By the time the last song had been sung, the child slept soundly on Nathan's shoulder.

They stood and merged into a crowd making a way toward the door at the rear of the sanctuary. A dozen townspeople greeted them.

Ella recognized that the men outnumbered females at least two to one. No wonder their meager group of women had been welcomed into this community with open arms.

"Mrs. Lantry?"

At a touch on her shoulder, she turned. The address had been for *her,* of course. A slender woman in a green dress and matching hat gave her a hesitant smile. "I'm Betsy Iverson. I couldn't help noticing your lovely voice this morning."

"Oh. Thank you," Ella said, caught by surprise.

"We have a choral group who sing for special occasions, and we'd love to have you come join our rehearsal this week. Thursday afternoon at two right here. Afterward, we go over to Minnie Oliver's for tea."

"Well." Ella had never sung, other than humming notes to learn a musical piece on the piano, and she'd never taken afternoon tea, but apparently these were the pastimes of the women of Sweetwater. She glanced at Nathan to find him observing her uncomfortable exchange. She raised an eyebrow in question. Was Betsy Iverson's invitation an acceptable event?

"It sounds like a good way to become acquainted with the ladies, and it's a pleasant afternoon diversion," he said, coming to her rescue.

She nodded. "All right then." She glanced back at Betsy. "Thank you. I'd love to join your gathering."

"Lovely. We'll look forward to getting to know you."

Nathan nodded approvingly.

Ella kept the smile on her face, despite all the assessing looks she received. Celeste emerged from the crowd, her new husband beside her. Ella wondered if her own expression was every bit as stupefied as Celeste's after the morning's events. She tried to keep her grasp on Celeste's hand from breaking any bones, but she was so glad to see her, she didn't want to let go.

"What a morning," Celeste said. "But church was nice, wasn't it?"

"Very," she replied, glancing at a stranger studying her over Celeste's shoulder.

"Come call on Celeste anytime," Paul Adams said from beside her. "She'd like your company."

"I will," Ella promised. She released Celeste's hand, and the couple moved toward the open doors.

"Will you take Grace's hand, please?" Nathan asked. "She barely comes up to the belt buckles in this crowd."

Ella turned readily and reached for Grace. Once out of doors, he guided Ella up to the buggy, and then held Robby up to her.

She fumbled with the child's sagging weight for a moment, arranging him on her lap and cradling his head against her breast. "This little fellow is surprisingly heavy."

Christopher and Grace settled themselves on the rear seat, and Nathan led the team toward his home.

Ella had been too distracted the evening before to notice the even brick streets they traveled or the neighborhood Nathan led them to. Most of the homes were more modest than Nathan's, but a few were equally as impressive. All were well-kept and painted in attractive colors or fresh white, with gardens and hedges and trees established. It was a far cry from Dodge City with its dusty streets and rows of saloons.

She'd known, of course, that Mrs. Fairchild's establishment had been a polished diamond among rough stones and that the clientele were businessmen living in Kansas purely for the monetary gain of the burgeoning cattle business, but never had it been as apparent as today.

"As soon as we've changed clothing, we'll set out our meal," Nathan said to her. "Afterward the children will take naps, and you and I will have a few hours together."

With a smile, she nodded.

As planned, they met in the kitchen after changing clothes. The children scrambled onto chairs to await their lunch, and Nathan glanced at her skirt and blouse. "Did you bring any aprons?"

She shook her head.

"Let's borrow one of Charlotte's." He found a faded apron in a drawer and unfolded it for her.

She slipped the bib over her head and wrapped the ties around her waist. Nathan stepped behind her, took the sashes from her hands, their fingers brushing, and tied it. He smelled good, like a blend of sandalwood and bay rum. From behind, he placed his hands on her shoulders and leaned forward where she could look up and meet his gaze. They stood like that for a moment, until Ella let her focus drop to his lips.

He released her and glanced at a note propped against the sugar bowl on a lower open shelf. "It seems we have a casserole to remove from the oven and bread to slice."

"I can slice bread," she offered.

He set the table and they shared an informal dinner right there at the kitchen table. "Robby will sleep through this meal and wake famished," Nathan told her.

"I'll save a plate of food for him," she offered.

"Jimmy Evans thinks you're going to be our mama," Christopher said.

Nathan laid down his fork.

Ella did the same. "Is Jimmy a friend of yours?"

Christopher shrugged. "He's a little bit of a friend."

"Do you want me to be your mother?" she asked.

Nathan appeared surprised by her question. Grace just blinked from one person to the next and chewed.

"I dunno," he replied with a shrug. "Richard Crandall's mama yells at him a lot, and she doesn't let him stay to play ball 'cause she says he has to do chores."

"I assure you I won't be yelling at you," she told him. She glanced at Nathan. "Does he have any chores?"

Nathan shook his head before locking his gaze on his son. "I've been thinking this will be the year that you help shovel the front walk and the area in front of the stable doors, though. You're getting to be a big strong boy."

"Shoveling snow will be *fun!*" he said.

"Most people don't get to choose their mothers or their children," Nathan pointed out. "You and Ella are able to choose if you want to be mother and son. No one is going to make you call her mother or love her. That's up to you."

His words tugged at Ella's heart. She still hadn't figured out how to be a wife. How was she supposed to know how to be a *mother,* too?

"But you must be respectful and kind," he added. "Do you understand?"

"Yes, sir." Christopher finished his bread and butter

unconcernedly. "May I read before nap time?" he asked.

"Of course," Nathan replied. "As long as you're quiet and don't disturb your sister or brother."

Nathan asked Ella to accompany them, then wiped Grace's face and hands and carried her up the stairs. She clung to his neck and stared over his shoulder as Ella followed. Ella had yet to hear her utter a word.

The children's room was long, with wooden shutters that closed over the inside of the windows. Nathan pulled them shut now, all except for the single panel he left slanted open near Christopher's bed. The boy removed his shoes, selected a book, and made himself comfortable.

Nathan took off Grace's tiny boots and tucked her under her covers. She stretched both arms toward him, and he bent over her bed to share a hug. "Rest well, buttercup."

She closed her eyes.

He moved to adjust the covers around Robby in another small bed, and then they slipped from the room, Nathan closing the door firmly.

"What would you like to do?" he asked.

She thought a moment. "Do you have a piano?"

He shook his head.

"Never mind then. I thought I could play for you."

"I should have an instrument so the children can learn," he said.

"I could teach them," she suggested brightly.

"That would be nice."

"I have a phonograph in one of the crates that came from the train depot. We could listen to the cylinders."

He nodded. "Those crates are on the sunporch. Let's go find your phonograph, and I'll carry it to the sitting room."

The spacious area he called a sunporch was an enclosed room on the back of the house with two walls of windows, one of which overlooked a gentle slope leading to a stream, easily identified by the strip of wooded area that wound across the landscape with the flow of the water.

"What a lovely place to live." Her breath caught. She hadn't meant to sound so emotional.

"When I selected this site, Sweetwater was still a row of tents and clapboard stores," he said while moving crates. She turned to look at him. He had rolled back his sleeves over corded forearms with a dusting of dark hair. "I had my heart set on building a house here. Raising a family." He paused to gaze out over the countryside. "Life takes unpredictable twists."

He meant his wife's death, obviously. Ella moved to the simple screen door that opened onto the yard. All she had to do was open that door and walk outside. No one would stop her.

She tested her freedom by flipping up the flimsy hook that held the door shut. She turned to look behind her and confirm that the door that led from the house to the porch was the one that locked for safety purposes.

"Something wrong?"

She shook her head.

"Even if someone broke that hook and eye and came into the porch, they couldn't get in the house," he assured her.

"I see that. I was just thinking how easy it would be to walk outside and wander down by those trees along the stream."

"That's why I keep the door hooked," he said. "Grace and Robby can't reach it. Christopher knows enough to stay away from the water."

Of course he thought of the children's safety. She thought only of the lack of restrictions. "I can walk out there anytime I like."

"Yes, of course," he replied. "Use wisdom, of course."

He found the phonograph and removed it from the crate. "I can set it up right out here, if you prefer."

She hadn't moved from the doorway. She turned and looked at him. "I'd like that very much."

He cleared a space on a table and positioned the phonograph. "I saw these at the exposition last summer and thought about getting one. Did you find this in Illinois?"

"I ordered it from a catalog." Ella located the cardboard tubes that held her Edison wax cylinders, placed one of them on the mandrel and wound the machine.

A tinny waltz emanated from the sound machine.

Nathan watched his beautiful new wife as she listened to the music and let her gaze drift back to the green landscape. She stood at the screen door, her slender form in the pale yellow blouse silhouetted by the afternoon sun turning the grass and trees to vivid shades of green.

She was an exquisite vision of perfection and femininity, her clear blue eyes alight with the pleasure and vitality of life. He thought of asking her to dance, but thought better of the idea.

Her exotic cinnamon and musk scent teased his senses. And when he looked at her mouth…he wanted to kiss her…kiss her until they were both puddles of hopeless need and blistering desire. But he knew better. The last thing he wanted was to see the sparkle fade from her eyes and the light of discovery and expectation leave her expression. Reality did that to a woman.

The music wound to a halt, the drone of an insect on a screen the only remaining sound. She turned and met his gaze. His heart surged up into his throat and threatened to stop for good.

Chapter Six

He'd only known her for a week, and already she created havoc with his common sense. She reminded him of a butterfly newly emerged from its cocoon, testing her wings on the breeze.

She smiled and his breath hitched in his chest. He was a fool. "Let's walk down by the stream," he suggested, knowing the idea would appeal to her.

She agreed, as he'd known she would and he led her out of doors, where he took her hand and they strolled across the grass. Her fingers were slim and delicate. He turned over her palm to study the soft pink skin. She was unaccustomed to work.

She gazed up at him, those blue eyes innocent and trusting. She had placed all her hopes and dreams in his care. Her happiness was a weighty responsibility...one he feared...one he treasured...but a duty he coveted.

They neared the bank of the stream, and she cast her

attention to the gently moving water. "Look," she said, releasing his hand to inch closer. "It's so clear you can see the stones beneath the surface."

"This is why the town was named Sweetwater," he told her.

"Oh, my!" she said excitedly. "See the little fish darting here and there?"

He nodded, but cared only to observe her delighted expression. She reminded him of his children on Christmas morning, their eyes aglow with wonder and excitement. All he'd done was walk her across his lawn, but she behaved as though he'd taken her on a grand adventure.

"Have you never seen fish before?" he asked.

"Only on a plate with lemon sauce," she replied. "A much larger variety, for certain."

He chuckled and she shot her gaze to his. "Where have you been, Ella, that you've never seen a fish?"

She turned away without reply, her gaze once again on the shimmering water. "I've been in a place much different from this."

"I meant no insult."

"None taken."

A few minutes passed, the sound of the gurgling water a pleasant backdrop to his thoughts. "You can take off your shoes and walk in the water, if it pleases you."

Taken by surprise at his suggestion, Ella glanced up at him. "Wouldn't that be unladylike?"

"Even if it was, there's no one here but the two of us."

"I don't know," she hedged.

"I'll join you."

"You?" She had trouble picturing it.

He sat and removed his boots, then tugged off his socks and rolled up his trouser legs, revealing long feet and corded ankles sprinkled with dark hair. He stood and waded out into the water. "The stones are smooth underfoot. It's safe."

Ella watched him, intrigued by the sparkle of the sun on the water and his feet rippling under the surface. She sat and removed her shoes, then hiked up her skirt and petticoat to roll down her stocking.

He stood planted in the stream, his dark gaze taking in her every move.

Ella tossed the stocking aside and reached to roll down the other, more slowly this time. He was definitely interested. She smiled to herself. Feet bare, she recognized the fascinatingly cool tickle of the grass under her soles. She stood, gathered the hem of her skirt above her knees and made her way to the edge of the water.

She walked in, the same as he had, shocked by the frigid temperature of the water. Chills ran up both legs and she sucked in a surprised breath. "It's *cold!*"

He laughed. "Did I forget to mention that?"

"You most certainly forgot to mention that." The stones were smooth, a little bit slippery, and the water was a brisk, yet gently lapping current against her calves. She loved the sensation, as well as the warm sun on her face…and the expression of the man watching her.

Something tickled her ankle, and she glanced down to discover a swarm of miniature fish.

"Oh!" She gasped in surprise and jumped to put all her weight on one foot and raise the other out of the water. While she teetered on a single foot, the fish promptly gathered around the remaining ankle. She leaped to the other foot, dropping her hem in the process and then grabbing it up, dripping wet, and raising it even higher than before. "The fish are biting me!"

Laughing, Nathan waded toward her, and she lunged for him, attempting to leap right up into his arms out of the water and away from the mysterious creatures.

He lost his balance and staggered to one side, grabbing her behind the knees and lifting her against his chest, while laboring to regain his footing.

He almost stabilized himself, but lost his balance, and a foot shot out from under him, plummeting them both into the stream.

The water here wasn't deep, but it was cold, and immediately soaked through Ella's clothing to her skin and turned her backside to ice. Nathan's sharp intake of breath revealed his shock, as well, but he sputtered and laughed.

Ella floundered to lunge her weight forward and stand, but her foot caught on the hem of her skirt and she plopped back into the water, this time splashing her face and hair and soaking a good portion of her blouse.

Now that she was caught in her wet skirts, Nathan laughed all the harder, helpless to do anything to aid her or himself. The hair plastered to his forehead dripped water, and his wet shirt molded to his chest. His teeth were white and even, and the corners of his eyes crinkled in merriment.

Ella had a fleeting image of him dressed formally the night they'd met and wondered what all those people at the party would think of their city attorney at this moment. His hearty laughter was contagious.

An unfamiliar pleasure rose up inside her and spilled over in a burst. She heard the sound, but couldn't reconcile it as coming from her. A full thirty seconds passed... a minute...yes, she was laughing. Laughing for all she was worth.

Almost frightened at the oddity, she caught herself and clapped a hand over her mouth.

Nathan's laughter faded, and his smile waned, his gaze dropping to her hand over her mouth, then her wet clothing.

She let her hand drop to her side and stared at him breathing hard, his eyes growing darker and his expression changing. A quick glance showed that her thin wet blouse had become transparent, and the icy water had done more than give her shivers.

Without thinking about the consequences, she sprang forward and took his face between her hands. She had only a second to register his startled expression before she covered his lips with hers and kissed him without restraint.

Chapter Seven

Everything about her new life was awkward and unfamiliar. She felt decidedly lost and inept. She couldn't cry. But she could find a recognizable foothold and cling to it for her security.

His mouth was warm and his arms radiated heat when they wrapped around her, the temperature a welcome contrast to the icy water and the icy cold seeping through her clothing. The enchanting pressure of his eager lips took her by surprise.

Against her fingertips his damp jaw was smoothly shaven, slick and warm. A startling flutter took up a beat in her stomach and spread to her chest, making it difficult to breathe.

She wanted to press closer, become a part of him and never lose this incredible new sense of security and feeble hope.

Nathan eased his lips from hers. He studied her eyes for a fleeting moment. "You're shivering."

She'd thought the trembling was inside.

He picked her up in his arms, securely this time, and carried her to the bank, where he climbed out of the water and set her down. "You might want to wring out your skirts."

She took a step away and sat on the grass to do as he'd suggested. He ineffectually squeezed water from the cuffs of his trousers. He picked up his shoes. "We'd better go back to the house and change into dry clothing."

Ella gathered her stockings and shoes and joined him.

That evening, Nathan called the family to join him in his study. The warmth of the day had waned, and he'd lit a fire. The room, filled with comfortable leather chairs and burgeoning cases of books, was pleasant and welcoming.

Christopher opened a box of miniature figures and set them up in some sort of formation on the stone slab that comprised the hearth. His accompanying noises alerted Ella that the figures were soldiers.

Grace settled two rag dolls on the footstool and fed them imaginary food from a tiny set of china dishes.

Robby dumped a bag of wooden blocks on the floor and stacked them into a tower, humming to himself.

"Grace hasn't spoken to me yet," Ella whispered to Nathan.

"She doesn't speak to me, either," he replied. "Sometimes I hear her talking to her dolls when she's alone in her room, though."

"Has she always been so silent?"

He nodded. "She was still a baby when Robby was born and her mother died. She cries when she's hurt or frightened, but she never asks for anything."

Ella studied the little girl. She was well cared for and had advantages many children didn't. Losing her mother had undoubtedly been traumatic, but it didn't explain her silence.

Ella settled on the floor near the footstool. "Do you suppose I could have tea, too?"

Grace looked her over skeptically before picking up a miniature cup and saucer and handing them to her. The child understood and responded, so there was nothing wrong with her hearing.

"Thank you. I don't suppose you have any cookies?"

Grace nodded and picked something invisible from the upholstered footstool and extended her fingers toward Ella as though she held a treat.

Ella pretended to take it and try a bite. "It's delicious. What kind of cookie is it?"

Grace merely tilted her head to the side as though she didn't know and went back to feeding her dolls.

"Definitely oatmeal with raisins," Ella said. "They're my favorites. How did you know that?"

Grace said nothing, but handed her another imaginary cookie.

Later, Ella accompanied Nathan when he tucked the children into their beds in the nursery. She studied the room, noting their books and toys and Grace's row of dolls. Ella had never had a doll. She'd had daytime lessons and voice lessons and practiced French in the evenings. She couldn't recall idle moments until her studies had ended at age sixteen and she'd been alone mornings while the household slept.

On a low round table sat some sort of boat with a roof, made of wood and painted to appear as though it had dozens of windows in the cabin area. On its deck and around the outside stood a couple dozen pairs of animals. She recognized the sheep and giraffe Robby had played with in church.

Nathan spoke softly to each of his offspring, reaching for a stuffed bear that Robby requested. By what stroke of fortune had these children been born to a man who took an active role in their care? She supposed she'd comprehended that other children had fathers. It was a natural fact that everyone had been sired by someone, but how many people knew a father like this? She never really considered it. As Nathan kissed his children, she wondered if Ansel Murdock had tucked in his children when they'd been young. During the past few years, where had he told his wife and sons he was going on Monday and Friday evenings?

The Lantrys were a lifetime away from everything she'd known. Living among them was like being dropped into a fairy tale.

Nathan turned down the wicks in the lamps and reached for her hand to lead her from the room.

What would she do if Nathan routinely left for evenings out?

A startling question loomed in her mind. Were there parlor houses and dinner clubs in Sweetwater?

"Would you like to keep me company for the rest of the evening?" he asked as they stood in the upstairs hall.

She nodded. "Yes."

"Perhaps you'd like to bring along a book or your needlework?"

She could sew enough to do a quick mend, but had never tried her hand at stitchery. "I'll read," she replied, quickly heading for her room to find a book.

Once they were again in his study, he said, "You may spend your evenings however you like, Ella."

"I like it in here," she replied. "As long as I'm not disturbing you."

"Of course you're not disturbing me." He settled on a leather armchair and glanced at her book. "What are you reading?"

"It's an account of an explorer named Champlain. He lived among the Huron Indians to study them. He adopted their language and customs, and became familiar with the landscape and water routes. His study of geography and Indian life inspired many men after him."

"Yes, I've heard of him." Nathan gestured for her to show him the book, and she handed it over. He glanced at the cover and then opened it. He raised his eyebrows. "It's printed in French."

She nodded. "Yes, Samuel de Champlain was a Frenchman."

"Yes, I know he was a Frenchman. My surprise was in the fact that you're reading the book in French."

She shrugged. "Many of my books are in French."

"You became fluent in French at Miss Haversham's?"

She took the book from him and settled on a nearby divan.

"That's a Roman divan," he told her, getting up and moving to show her how to lift the upholstered arm. "Raise either arm until the ratchet disconnects and then you can lower it to a position so you can recline."

"How ingenious," she replied.

He left the arm lowered.

"You could sit beside me," she suggested.

Nathan studied her uplifted face, the delicate curve of her cheek and the question in her eyes. Looking at her increased his pulse rate and created havoc with his common sense. That afternoon had proven his supreme lack of resistance where she was concerned. He'd given his word and resolved to give their developing relationship six months.

Now, thinking about the unbearable length of time he'd carved made the wait seem like an eternity. But he couldn't sit across the room avoiding her for the next six months. Part of developing a relationship was earning her trust.

He eased onto the divan only inches from her. "Would you like to bring down your books and keep them on a shelf in here? That way they'd be nearby in the evening."

"I'd like that. And you are welcome to read any that catch your eye."

"I don't read French."

"They're not all in French."

"You're welcome to mine, as well."

Her gaze lifted and she scanned the spines on the wall of bookcases. "Any?"

"Of course."

She got up and crossed to scan titles, pausing with her finger on one. *"Ravenshoe."* Sliding out the volume, she opened it to the first page.

"It's a character's name," he supplied.

She replaced it. *"Lady Audley's Secret,"* she read from another.

"It's a sensation novel. I'm afraid my reading tastes aren't as refined as yours," he apologized. "There are classics if you look."

"What is a sensation novel?"

"Plots with subjects shocking to some. If you choose to read it, don't let on to the good ladies of Sweetwater."

"What are the shocking subjects?"

"I don't care to spoil the story for you."

"You are more likely to entice me."

He'd married a champagne drinker who didn't faint at the thought of impropriety. "No French explorers in the lot. A seemingly perfect domestic lady attempts to commit murder. The character has also committed bigamy and abandoned her child."

"I believe I'll read this one first then," she said with a grin.

He tilted his head. "I warned you."

She sat down beside him, the book unopened. "Warning taken."

"Tell me about your family," he suggested. "We have a lot to talk about, don't we?"

"There's not much to say about them." She adjusted her skirts.

"What did your father do?"

Celeste had been right about this. During their journey to Wyoming, Celeste had brought up the subject of planning what to tell the people they met. *"People don't just fall out of the sky,"* she'd said. *"We have to have background stories ready."*

And so whenever they'd had time alone, the women had compared their ideas for what they would say when questions were asked.

What *did* fathers do? "He was a banker. A stockholder, actually. He belonged to a gentleman's club and attended St. Mark's Episcopal Church."

"And your mother?"

More lies. Would it always be lies she was telling to this man? "I didn't know my mother well." And that was as close to the truth as possible. But he waited for more. "She died when I was very young. That's why I went to Miss Haversham's."

"Any brothers or sisters?"

That would depend on who her father had been, but

she would never know. "None. What about you? Do you have brothers and sisters?"

"I have an older sister and two younger brothers," he answered.

"You all lived together when you were young?"

He nodded. "Oh, yes. Our bickering drove my poor mother to distraction, but she's a saint."

"She's still alive?"

"And still living in the family home in Philadelphia. We will visit before the end of the year. She'd enjoy seeing the children, and I'd like for her to meet you."

She nodded, unable to imagine meeting his mother.

"My father's only been gone a few years," he continued. "He was a judge. That's how I came to go to law school; but then the war came along, so I never practiced."

"You fought during the war?"

"Fought in Missouri early on. Later I was with Sheridan when we trapped Jubal Early's army on our way to Waynesboro. We were the regiment that blocked Lee's escape at Appomattox, forcing the Northern Virginia army's surrender. After the war, the General wanted me to accompany him to Prussia, where he was sent to advise during that war in 70, but I'd seen enough destruction." All that seemed a lifetime ago. "I was intent on building something, and I'd never forgotten this place. So I finished my law degree, purchased a railcar full of lumber and asked a young woman to marry me.

"Sweetwater was a tent town then. Only a few buildings existed. But the town was right along the path of the Union Pacific as the rails expanded westward. I discovered I could sell my lumber for far more than I'd purchased it, so I did. Sold it and had more sent from Colorado. I posted notices in the major newspapers, and a few merchants and even a dentist threw in on the new venture. There's nothing like settling the land and watching something grow. Wasn't long before Sweetwater was a respectable town."

More comfortable now that she'd turned the focus back on him, Ella listened to his story with interest. Nathan was impressively enterprising and ambitious. She was surprised to learn he owned a lumberyard.

"Is that where you work during the day?"

"No, I have people who run it for me. I work in an office at the municipal building."

She pictured everything about his stories, everything except one thing. "What was your wife's name?"

He paused a moment before replying. "Deborah."

"Do your children look like her?"

"Robby looks the most like her. Christopher reminds me of my father, and Grace looks like my sister, Vanessa."

"Christopher looks like you," she told him.

He nodded. "Many said I looked like my father."

She didn't want to pry into a hurtful subject, but she was curious. "Is it painful to talk about your wife?"

"I have a lot of regrets," he answered, which didn't address her question.

She didn't pry.

"Deborah was unprepared for a life far away from

everything she'd known in Philadelphia," he went on, surprising her and holding her interest. "I built her a beautiful home, started a planning council and brought in a doctor and a teacher. Soon there were churches and schools." He shrugged. "But this isn't the big city, and the social activities can't compare. She missed her family." He glanced at Ella.

Nathan had a respectable background and a commendable war record. His ambition and vision had sparked accomplishments for which he could be proud. But beneath the handsome exterior and the successful businessman, she sensed a vulnerability that spoke to her untried heart. Now his first words to her made sense. "When we met, you asked why I'd traveled West and warned me this place wasn't what I was accustomed to."

"Deborah didn't complain, but she was never happy here. I took her away from her family and her home."

"I have no family or home, and Sweetwater is far better than where I came from," she assured him. Whatever he imagined about her, she didn't want him thinking she was unsatisfied with his home or the way he had welcomed her.

He shifted on the sofa to look more fully into her eyes. She offered him a warm smile.

He raised his hand and stroked her cheek with the backs of his fingers. "You're incredibly beautiful."

Her gossamer bubble of pleasure burst with the disappointment of that familiar endearment from his lips. *Beautiful* was nothing she hadn't heard a hundred times.

It meant nothing. "Isn't it true that beauty is in the eye of the beholder?"

He slid his fingers into the hair at her nape. "There isn't a beholder on this earth who wouldn't agree."

Encouraged, she slowly leaned toward Nathan, keeping her expression soft, her body language yielding. "I'm very happy to be right here, Nathan."

As she'd hoped, he leaned toward her and their lips met. It was gentle, his kiss, undemanding...sweet. Like no other kiss she'd ever experienced, not even like the first kiss they'd shared—or like the impulsive one in the stream that day—because this time she'd been prepared for the contact to be enjoyable.

She reached to skim her fingertips along his jaw and frame his warm cheek with her palm.

Nathan slid closer on the divan to take her shoulders into his embrace and hold her more tightly. She liked the taste of him, the feel of his arms around her, his clean scent. She liked everything about his kiss...particularly the way he made her feel as though she was someone special, someone deserving of his attention.

Inexplicably, a question came to her, a thought that disturbed her and stole a measure of her joy. Had Nathan kissed other women since his first wife's death? Would she care? Had he taken a lover...or visited a parlor house? It was the nature of men to sate their basic physical needs, and he was a man like any other. Would it matter to her if he had?

Ella wished she hadn't thought of the possibility. Considering his intimate exploits made her an even bigger hypocrite.

When had it started to matter that he want her for any reason other than securing her position as his wife? Why should she care if he had bedded a hundred women? Since when did it pain her to hear a man compliment her beauty? She had come all this way to find a respectable position and live her life freely, and that was still her mission.

But something had happened since she'd met and married Nathan. Something she couldn't have anticipated or planned for. Now she cared what this man thought of her.

She moved away enough to speak. "Will you walk me upstairs to my room?"

"All right," he said, his voice gruff.

She took his hand and got to her feet. He stood beside her, towering over her and gazing down into her eyes. She turned and led the way up the stairs, pausing outside her room. "Will you light the lamps?"

She opened the door, and stood aside for him to enter.

Chapter Eight

He found the matches and lit a wall sconce and the oil lamp on her bureau.

"It's so quiet here at night," she said softly. "In the city I heard more commotion."

He stood, facing the door, but without moving toward it. "I suppose it takes some getting used to."

"I suppose it does."

He turned to look at her, his gaze dropping from her face to caress her form beneath her clothing. "Good night, Ella."

"Good night."

Nathan closed her door and strode down the hall, his footsteps muffled on the carpet runner. He returned to his study and banked the fire.

She was in his blood, that woman. Everything about her, the sound of her voice stating the most innocent fact, her intoxicating scent, the sheen of her lustrous, dark hair and the curves beneath her clothing, everything combined to set him on fire. How would he last six months with her nearness an exquisite torment? What had he been thinking?

For safety, he set an iron grate in front of the fireplace and headed up to his room. He lit a lamp, then deliberately walked to his bureau and opened the top drawer to pull out a flat wooden box. Setting it on top of the chest of drawers, he opened it and took a breath before picking up the wedding portrait of himself and Deborah.

He could answer his own question of what he'd been thinking. He'd rushed into marriage the first time, that's why he'd vowed to take things more slowly with Ella.

Deborah had been so young, so unprepared for the life he'd unwittingly led her into. Filled with starry-eyed dreams and lofty expectations, she'd followed along, believing that every young girl's dream of a husband and family was coming true to her liking.

She'd taken one look at the sorry excuse for a town, and disappointment had swept her features into numb shock. He'd promised that they'd only be at the hotel until their house was built, and then they'd furnish it with all the comforts of home. And they had.

Turning, he studied the lustrous dark woodwork, the walnut, four-poster bed and the tall, hand-carved chifforobe. The entire house was filled with beautiful furniture, luxurious carpets and draperies. Deborah had been appreciative, but she'd never seemed at home. All the material things in the world couldn't buy a person's happiness.

She'd loved him, he was certain, but she'd reserved her affections for the children. She'd been an outstanding mother and a loving caregiver, preferring to stay home and keep the children near. He'd encouraged her to make friends and join the ladies' groups, but she'd attended rarely and then only to please him.

The reminder of her discontent would serve to quell his lusty ideas about his new wife. He set the frame on top of the bureau and took a long hard look at Deborah's deceptively serene face, reminded of the discontent that eroded every hope he'd ever had about their marriage.

This new marriage was nothing like that, and he would keep it that way. Ella had chosen to come to Sweetwater on her own. She'd set her sights on a husband before she'd ever met him, so he hadn't pulled her away from anywhere or anyone preferable. Still, coming here was a big adjustment, and taking a husband an even bigger one.

Yes, Ella welcomed his kisses, but the two of them had yet to advance to the reality of intimate dealings between man and wife. She was still caught up in the romance of marriage. The last thing he wanted to rush was her disillusionment when she discovered the physical aspect. Memories of Deborah were all it took to assure him he was using wisdom with his choice to wait. In the end, time would be his friend.

"I owe you an apology," Nathan said to her the following morning. He'd been waiting in the hall when she'd exited her room in hopes of reaching the kitchen before the meal was prepared and everyone seated at the table.

"Whatever for?" she asked.

"Our marriage came up unexpectedly, and I didn't plan for a honeymoon—or even time away from my job. I promise we'll take a trip as soon as I can arrange something."

She'd read a few newspapers with wedding announcements and recognized now that newly wedded couples often took a holiday after the ceremony. "I know you weren't prepared," she answered. "I didn't expect a trip."

"I understand if you're disappointed, but we can plan something together this way."

"Nathan," she said, resting her hand on the sleeve of his serge suit coat. "I assure you I wasn't expecting a honeymoon trip. I don't need a trip. I traveled quite a distance to get here. I'm not in a hurry to leave."

"But it would be a pleasant diversion if we plan a honeymoon together?" he asked.

"Yes, of course."

"Anywhere you like," he assured her.

"All right. We'll talk about it. I hoped to help Charlotte with breakfast this morning. Am I too late?"

"No, but perhaps you won't mind helping Grace instead. Mrs. Shippen won't be here for another half hour. The boys are up and dressed, but Grace was more difficult to wake."

"Yes," she answered immediately, but the thought terrified her. "I'll go check on her."

Nathan thanked her and headed down the stairs.

Ella approached the nursery, where she tapped on the partially open door. "Grace, are you awake?"

Hesitantly, she entered. All three beds were empty and unmade. Puzzled, she saw no one, but then heard a sound that came from behind a privacy screen. Moving toward it, she walked around the side and stopped short.

Grace, hair mussed, nightdress hiked, sat on a miniature wooden chair that housed a chamber pot. She gazed up at Ella with wide sleepy blue eyes.

"Oh." Ella took a step back. "I didn't know where you were, but I see you're awake."

Grace unconcernedly scratched her head and finished her business, then stood and padded back into the room, where she pointed to an armoire constructed of golden oak.

Ella opened it to discover an array of dresses. "Do you want to select your dress for today?"

Grace touched the hem of a blue garment, and Ella took it from its wooden hanger. "It's lovely." She opened narrow drawers on the side of the piece of furniture and located underclothing. "Let's see if you have warm water."

Grace stood beside the low washstand as though waiting.

Ella tested the water in the pitcher, finding it warm, then poured some into the bowl and handed Grace the dry washrag.

Grace looked at it and handed it back.

Ella soaked and wrung it and extended it again.

Grace just looked at her.

Finally comprehending that she was supposed to wash the little girl, she did so. Grace blinked as the cloth touched her face, but she studied Ella solemnly.

"There." Ella hung the cloth to dry and helped her change into her clothing, kneeling to work on her stockings and help her with her shoes. At last, she looked at Grace's tangled hair and sighed. "Where's your hairbrush?"

Grace pointed to a bureau drawer.

"All right then." Ella located the items she needed and set about gently working knots from her hair and dressing it in two neat braids. She kept up a steady stream of one-sided dialogue as she worked, finally standing back to look at her handiwork.

Grace was a lovely child, ivory-skinned and rosy-cheeked. She gave Ella a bashful smile that created dimples just like Christopher's. "All finished. You did well at selecting your own clothing,"

They descended the stairs together and Grace led the way to the dining room. "There's my pretty girl," Nathan said to his daughter.

Ella cringed at the comment. He meant well, and it was true, Grace was a fair child, but emphasis on appearance made Ella uncomfortable. In Ella's experience, praise for beauty only reduced a person to an object for another's pleasure.

Once they'd eaten breakfast, Nathan wished Ella a good day, kissed Grace and Robby and left to take

Christopher to school and go to his office. Ella helped Charlotte with the dishes.

"What is the normal routine for the remainder of the day?" she asked when Mrs. Shippen arrived.

"The children occupy themselves with their toys while I make beds and gather the laundry," she answered. "At noon I prepare them lunch, and then they nap in the afternoon."

"I'm not sure what's expected of me," Ella said with discomfort.

"I was here when the first Mrs. Lantry was alive," Mrs. Shippen said. "She occupied herself with the children most of the time. Otherwise she read and sewed. On rare occasions she joined the other wives for luncheons or tea."

Grace and Robby seemed surprised to see Ella enter the nursery. Robby set down his wooden block and ran over to her. "Read to Robby?"

"I'd love to read to you. But let's make your beds first."

He did his best to help her pull up and straighten sheets and blankets. He turned and grabbed a rag doll and struggled to climb on Grace's bed, mussing it again, but proudly placed the doll on her pillow and climbed back down. "There!"

Ella commended him and nonchalantly smoothed the spread where he'd mussed it. Once the beds were made, she let him select a book, sat on the nearby rocker and read aloud.

Mrs. Shippen arrived, surprised to find the beds

made. "You made your own bed, too," she said. "Mr. Lantry makes his, as well, so my morning chores are getting lighter."

Her observation pointed out that the woman knew Nathan and Ella slept in separate rooms, but her tone didn't indicate surprise or disapproval.

"Let me know if there's anything else I can do," Ella offered.

Robby and Grace continued to bring her books. Finally, she suggested they put on sweaters and go out of doors for a walk. The children were appreciative of her attention and the unusual change in their schedule. They must have grown bored playing in their room most of the day, and she was glad to broaden their activities.

Robby's antics made her laugh and Grace's silent acceptance touched her. She thought of all the places she could have ended up, even had she somehow married a rancher back in Kansas, and knew she couldn't have found a better home or even a halfway respectable position that compared. The thoughts had her thinking about Celeste and the other girls and wondering how they fared this first week of their new lives.

Ella wasn't a dreamer. She knew better than to imagine situations that could never come to pass. But being here was real. By some amazing stroke of fate, she had landed in a place she didn't deserve, married to an exceedingly gentle and decent man. Nathan was kind to the household help. He loved his children, and had been nothing less than a gentleman where Ella was concerned.

She liked it here, and she liked this family. She would do whatever it took to stay and make herself invaluable.

That afternoon while the children slept, she insisted on peeling potatoes, though Charlotte had to show her how, and then darted curious glances at her the entire while. Afterward Ella selected a book and got a blanket from a stack in her closet, and carried them down beside the stream.

She spread the blanket and sat, listening to the remarkable sounds of the outdoors. After several minutes the birds resumed their songs and chirps. The breeze rustled through the leaves of the cottonwoods in a song more melodic than anything she had ever played on the piano. She closed her eyes and listened. The sun warmed her face, probably encouraging freckles at this very moment, but she didn't care. She'd never had the privilege of being left to her own devices for a day.

Her thoughts traveled to the previous day, to Nathan's encouragement to remove her shoes and stockings, and their playful, somewhat disastrous foray into the water that had led to a kiss she would never forget.

Ella had forgotten a lot of kisses. She had deliberately cast a great deal of her past out of her mind. But she wanted to cling to her memories with Nathan because they were the only pure and real experiences she'd known.

That she enjoyed his kisses may have been the most shocking discovery of her lifetime. What she'd intended as a ploy for her security had transformed into something she'd never expected—or wanted. Enjoying his kisses wasn't a comfort. It frightened her as few things could.

She opened her eyes and studied the puffy white clouds changing shapes in the blue sky. For the first time she acknowledged being a part of a universe so big that she felt small and insignificant...but breathtakingly alive.

The complete lack of restrictions was the most liberating feeling she'd ever known. She'd chosen a new destiny—to become a different person. Her previous life seemed a million miles away.

Yes, she was going to do everything she could to be the person Nathan and his children needed. She was, after all, Ella Lantry. She desired nothing more than to be worthy of his respect and his good name. She wouldn't let her husband down.

By Thursday, Ella could no longer wait to know how Celeste was faring in her new home. Over breakfast she brought up the subject of a visit to Nathan. "I'd like to call on Celeste, if it still meets with your approval."

He cast her a curious look. "Apparently you were restricted at Miss Haversham's, but you don't need my permission to leave the house or call on your friends, Ella. You're due for a day of socializing."

"I was invited to join the ladies' choir rehearsal, but I don't think I'm ready for that just yet. I can do that next week, when I'm more settled."

"Of course," he answered. "Whatever pleases you."

"I can take the children with me to visit Celeste," she offered.

She'd cared for them alone the previous day, while Mrs. Shippen enjoyed a day off.

"Not unless you have a burning desire to keep two small children entertained and out of mischief instead of visiting with your friend," he told her. "You're due for a day to yourself. Just enjoy seeing your friend."

Uncertain of Celeste's situation, she decided perhaps it was best she go alone the first time. The driver Nathan sent called for her midmorning. The fellow, whose name was Pete Driscoll, was a quiet sort, leading the horse along a well-traveled road.

Ella enjoyed the scenery, asking Mr. Driscoll to stop once so she could pick a bouquet of delicate lavender flowers. He helped her back up to her seat without comment, and delivered her to the Adams ranch well before noon.

Corrals and outbuildings littered the land, and a small one-story house sat near a stand of trees. To the west of the house, Celeste turned from a clothesline where she'd been hanging what looked like curtains. She spotted Ella climbing down and hurried to greet her. "Gab—" she began, and then caught herself. "Ella. What a wonderful surprise!"

She wore a plain dress and a white apron. She'd braided her black hair and it hung down her back in a thick plait. Her simple attire and this humble scene were unfamiliar to Ella, but Celeste's eyes sparkled and her face was alight with pleasure.

"I wanted to see you," Ella said and extended the bouquet of wildflowers before accepting the brief hug the young woman lavished upon her.

"Mr. Lantry asked me to wait for ya," the driver said. "I'll water the horse and find 'im some grass."

"Thank you," Ella replied.

Celeste took her arm and led her toward the house. "Come in and I'll make tea. I made a cake, and I want you to try it."

The kitchen was small, but adequate, with two long windows that opened onto the side yard, where a garden flourished. Celeste stood the flowers in a glass bottle she filled with water. "Paul said these are shooting stars," she told Ella, pointing to the lavender blooms. "I don't know what the pink or white ones are."

She poked around in the stove and added a few sticks to get the logs burning hot, then poured water from a pail into a kettle and set it on a burner. "Isn't this just a stitch, me making tea and cakes? Oh, hang your hat up over there."

Ella hung her hat and shawl on a peg beside the door, then took a seat.

Celeste uncovered a lopsided cake and cut a slice. "I make all the meals for Paul and me. He hasn't complained yet." She gave a half laugh. "He's had reason, though, believe me. I didn't know a sack of flour from a coffee bean until this week. But he's so patient. And he explains things without getting upset. He hasn't so much as lifted his voice, let alone a fist."

The news gave Ella a sense of relief. She tasted the cake and found it a little dry, but not terrible.

"Your tea will wash it down," Celeste told her, as though guessing her thoughts.

"I peeled potatoes," Ella told her.

"I never knew potatoes grew like that, did you?" Celeste asked. "Have you seen a turnip yet?"

Ella shook her head.

"And eggs! Goodness, I have to wrestle them away from the chickens!" The kettle boiled and she poured water over tea in a chipped pot, and then sat near Ella at the table. "But it's all worth it—the cooking and sweeping the floor every day and pulling weeds from the garden. He treats me like I'm—like I'm *special*." Though they were alone, she lowered her voice near a whisper. "He's gentle in the bed department—asks my permission, then questions if I like every little thing. He goes at it a couple of times a night, and Ella, he never had a woman before me, can you believe it? But he's just so sweet about it, and he holds me afterward."

She paused in her rush to tell Ella everything and got tears in her eyes.

Ella's own eyes smarted, and she swallowed hard to compose her emotions.

"I never knew there was a man like him," Celeste said, her voice thick with tears. "All I ever knew were cowhands in a hurry to get back to their card games and drunks and cheating husbands and those that wanted something their wives wouldn't do for them."

Ella nodded her understanding. She'd never known,

either—never imagined there were kind and courteous men, men who loved their children, men who put a woman's needs above their own.

Celeste poured hot tea into two cups and set one before Ella. "Is Mr. Lantry tender like that?"

Ella spooned sugar into her cup and stirred. "He's patient with his children, and has been nothing but polite and considerate."

"And he's a gentleman in the bedroom, too?"

Ella gave a hesitant shrug and let her gaze touch on everything on the table before lifting it to the other woman's face.

Celeste raised her eyebrows and her eyes widened. "You *haven't?*"

Chapter Nine

〰〰〰

"It's puzzling, I know," Ella said with a shake of her head. "He wants to have a courtship first."

"You'd better move past that right quick," Celeste told her with obvious concern. "Paul told me our marriage was consummated and legal after that first time. I had to ask him to explain, because I had no idea, but it seems there's still a chance to call the whole thing off if the husband and wife haven't put the final seal on things."

Ella stared at her. "Surely he's not holding out in case he changes his mind about me."

"Maybe he has his reasons." Celeste sipped her tea.

Ella picked up her cup. Nathan hadn't given her any indication that their marriage might not work out. Granted she wasn't familiar with household chores or cooking or…well, with anything for that matter; but she'd shown him she was willing to learn and do her part. "A piano is being delivered soon," she said. "When it arrives, I'll teach the children to read music and play."

"How are you getting on with the children?"

"Quite well. His daughter doesn't speak." She went on to share about the little ones. Some time later Paul arrived, greeted Ella warmly, and Celeste prepared him sandwiches and poured him a glass of buttermilk.

He ate his meal, then stood and thanked Celeste.

"You're welcome," she replied with a smile Ella had never seen before. The couple exchanged a private look.

Ella had the impression that if she hadn't been there, Paul would have kissed his wife...or perhaps more.

"Pleasure to see you, ma'am," he told Ella with a nod, then plucked his hat from a hook and exited the house.

Ella glanced at Celeste, surprised by the expression on her face as she watched him leave, and relieved that so far this match had truly been a good one.

They talked about their church experience and Celeste asked about the house and the staff. She made them each a sandwich, and after another cup of tea, Ella thanked her and headed for home.

On the way back, Ella thought about what she'd heard and seen. She asked Pete to stop again, so she could gather more of the shooting stars to take home. The man cheerfully dropped her off at the house, put the buggy in the carriage house and returned the horse to the livery.

Ella changed clothing and stewed about a marriage consummation while she helped Charlotte get out plates and prepare the evening meal. The wildflowers held a prominent position in the center of the table. She'd never had the impression that Nathan was holding back because of doubts about her or that their union might not work out. He'd seemed genuinely concerned that it was her tender sensibilities he was protecting.

Thinking that there was the slightest risk their marriage might not yet be legal gave her more cause to be concerned for her security. With every fiber of her being, she wanted to stay.

Lightning flashed beyond the windows of Nathan's study that evening. He rose and tugged the drapes closed.

"Is there a storm?" Christopher asked.

"It's just a spring rain," Nathan replied.

Grace's gaze traveled to the closed drapery and back to Nathan. She got up and darted to the window, where she parted the panels and stared out into the night.

"Just rain," Nathan told her. He glanced at Ella. "We received an invitation. The Crandalls are holding a Spring Gala next Saturday."

"What exactly is a Spring Gala?" Ella asked.

"An excuse to have a get-together with bouquets of flowers everywhere." He grinned. "And an opportunity for those in the community who haven't yet met you to do so."

Grace returned from the window and leaned into Nathan's lap, attempting to climb. He sat straighter and helped her up, where she made herself comfortable.

"It's nearly bedtime, buttercup," he told her.

She pointed to the bookshelves.

"What is it you want?" Ella asked, hoping for a reply.

Grace pointed again.

"I wish we knew what she wanted," Ella said to Nathan.

The little girl jumped down from his lap, ran to the bookcase and stood on tiptoe to reach the volume she wanted. The children's books were within easy reach on the lower shelves. She brought her selection back to Nathan and backed up so he'd lift her.

Ella had to admit the little girl got her point across without speaking.

Nathan opened the book and read the story. Ella was listening, watching Nathan's expressions and Grace's rapt face when she noticed the touch on her forearm. She glanced at Robby.

"Up?" he asked.

Surprised, she lifted him onto her lap and settled him so he could watch his father read. "I see, too!" he interrupted.

Nathan patted the divan beside him. Ella got up, carrying Robby, and moved to sit beside him so Robby could see the pictures. Her shoulder fit right below Nathan's, their upper arms molded together.

The mantel clock chimed a melodious sound, drawing her attention to the time. Her mind carried her back to evenings in Dodge, and the contrast in what she was doing now compared to what she'd have been doing had she stayed. What she'd done all of those evenings at Madame Fairchild's.

Mondays and Fridays had been Ansel's of course, but on Thursdays, one of the girls had a client who paid to have her *watch*. Ella hadn't known anything different. Those experiences had been normal—and until now she hadn't questioned normal.

She had often played the piano for the gathering, pretending not to notice any interaction between the girls and their gentlemen before they headed upstairs.

Hearing Celeste talk about Paul today, learning more about Nathan and seeing how lovingly these youngsters were treated—all of it pointed out just how sordid her past had been. Every day showed her more reasons to be grateful she was no longer in Kansas. And more reason to make certain she never returned to a life like that.

Robby was a lapful, but she appreciated his weight and his little boy wiggles and laughs. He leaned forward to point to a drawing on the pages and then turned to Ella with a question in his eyes.

"It's a frog," she told him.

"Wa-a-a-a-a-pft!" he said with his lips pursed and his chin tucked down, imitating a croak.

She laughed, and he burst into giggles.

Ella's eyes burned with unshed tears at the joy she experienced knowing the three young Lantrys were loved and that they had a bright future ahead of them. Nathan would stop at nothing to protect them and see to their education and happiness. These were her first glimpses of the advantages and innocence she had missed out on.

She'd never truly understood the depth of her childhood hardship until now.

That recognition dredged up a deep sadness and a longing for something that could never be replaced.

"Time to prepare for bed," Nathan said, interrupting her thoughts.

Robby jumped down and ran for the hall. Christopher picked up his toys before following. Grace wrapped her arms around Nathan's neck and waited for him to stand and carry her.

"Are all daughters daddy's girls?" Nathan asked with a grin.

She replied with only a smile. She knew nothing of daddies.

Once the children were washed and changed and tucked into their beds, the two adults returned to his study and Nathan offered her a glass of sherry. "Did you have a pleasant visit today?"

"Indeed. Celeste is doing well," she told him. "She seems quite content with Mr. Adams."

"News is Tom Bradbury is seeing your friend, Miss Kellie. Tom works at the bank and has a place on the street just east of here."

This Bradbury fellow must be well-to-do then. "Another admirable friend of yours?"

He nodded. "A fine upstanding citizen, Tom is."

It didn't surprise her that Lena had set her sights on a man who was probably the second wealthiest in town.

Ella carried her glass to the window and pulled a

drape panel aside to look out at the night. Drops of rain glistened on the windowpanes.

"Are you lonely here?"

His voice so near surprised her. She looked over her shoulder to find him disturbingly close, casually holding his glass, his gaze on the night. "No. Of course not."

"Will you tell me—if you ever feel lonely?"

"I doubt I will have occasion. The house is filled with activity in the evening. During the day Grace and Robby are good company."

"Grace doesn't talk," he remarked.

"That will change," she assured him.

"But you would tell me?" he insisted. "A person can be lonely in a sea of people and activity."

His concern touched her. "Yes, I would tell you. Because you have asked me." She turned to face him, letting the curtain fall back. "Are *you* lonely?"

He glanced at the liquid in his glass. "I didn't realize it, but I was...before you came."

"And now?"

He raised his head. "Now I have you."

"You barely know me."

He tilted his head. "I know enough. You're smart. And sensitive. And I've never seen anyone who appreciates learning new things or who gives her whole heart to each day the way you do. Sometimes I recognize that you're as innocent as one of the children, and the next moment your eyes or something you say reflects the pain of a person who has lived a long difficult life. You're a puzzle."

"I'm not complicated," she denied with a shake of her head.

"But you're a mystery."

She sipped her sherry. "I'm not attempting to be mysterious."

A clap of thunder startled her, and she took a step away from the window, toward him.

"Are you afraid of storms?" he asked.

The thunder had merely surprised her, but immediately, she remembered Celeste's words about making their marriage legal. "Well...honestly—" she gazed up at him "—I'm embarrassed to admit that lightning and thunder frighten me." She took another step closer to Nathan.

He took her glass and set both on a nearby table before turning back to enfold her in his arms. "There's nothing to fear. You're safe here."

Ella rested her cheek against the front of his shirt. He'd removed his jacket after dinner, so when she reached for his upper arm, only the soft fabric of his linen shirt separated her from solid muscle and warm skin. She closed her eyes and experienced the masculine scents of starch and shaving soap that were uniquely his.

She wasn't afraid of storms; never had been. Fear didn't come from what went on in the heavens; it came from what went on behind closed doors. The thought of outliving her usefulness and beauty and ending up like her mother was what terrified her. That's why she was here. Her keen sense of self-preservation precluded all other fears.

The hand he'd placed at the small of her back moved in reassuring circles. He raised his other to play with the hair at her nape, sending a shiver down her spine.

Lifting her head from its resting place, she studied him. His eyes were dark, but not brown or black. They were a deep hazel, with flecks of green and fringed by dark lashes. He had kind eyes that softened his otherwise stern features and well-defined lips.

"You're safe here," he said.

"Yes, I believe I am," she answered. As long as he never learned the truth about her.

Ella stroked his hard biceps, then his shoulder through the crisp fabric, letting her fingertips trail down the front of his shirt.

Beneath her touch, his chest muscles tensed. He lowered his eyelids briefly, and when he opened his eyes again, his hooded gaze riveted on her mouth.

"You're welcome to kiss me," she offered, then added, "Husband."

Desire flashed in his eyes, but with the restraint of a saint, he waited

Ella had seen her opportunity, and not to be dissuaded by his puzzling hesitation, she said more boldly, "Kiss me, Nathan."

He lowered his head and covered her mouth with his, and she welcomed the contact in yet another surprising discovery. She liked kissing him. A lot. He tasted hot and sweet, and the sheer pleasure stole her breath. Ella closed her eyes and gave herself over to the magical experience, reaching up to cradle his jaw.

At her touch against his face, he angled his head for a deeper, more thorough kiss, and she would have whimpered if she'd had the strength or the breath. Her knees quivered, and she clung to him.

Nathan supported Ella's weight easily, welcomed it in fact. Everything about her was delicate and soft and… and unbelievably arousing. She was the most generous woman he'd ever known, relentlessly giving of herself and her time. He strove only to hold himself in reserve, while she gave selflessly. The contrast shamed him. He shouldn't be taking advantage of her this way, but he couldn't resist.

He nipped at her generous bottom lip, traced the seam of her lips with his tongue, and she parted them in enthusiastic welcome. To his surprise and pleasure, she returned the bold kiss, taking the encounter to a hotter, more intense level. His desire for her hadn't needed fuel to burn at this white-hot fever.

It took a few seconds to realize the thundering wasn't in his head or his body, but rather the force of the storm gaining intensity outside the windows.

Ella pulled back enough to whisper, "May I stay with you tonight?"

"Ella—" he began.

"I'll feel safe with you," she interrupted.

How could he deny her anything? "If you wish," he replied.

Resting her palm on his chest, she studied him. "You'll wait outside my door while I change?"

"I'll wait," he promised.

She stood near while he banked the fire and turned out the lamps, then he took her hand and led her up the stairs.

"I'll only be a moment," she assured him. "I'll leave the door ajar." He waited in the hall, the rustle of her clothing setting his skin on fire.

She returned in a luminous white nightdress, and he took her hand so he wouldn't be tempted to touch her through the fabric. She'd be naked underneath, and there wasn't enough of the silky covering to hide or protect her.

He opened the door to his room, and she entered ahead of him in the darkness. "You take the bed," he offered.

He could recline in the overstuffed chair while she slept.

"I can't take your bed if you're not going to sleep," she said. "You need your rest for work tomorrow." She took a step toward the door. "I'll just go to my own room."

"No."

The word stopped her and she turned to face him.

"Stay," he said.

"All right." In the darkness, she peeled back the coverlet and sheet and climbed into his bed.

Nathan's heart pounded so hard she had to have heard it. He partially disrobed, leaving his trousers on, and moved to the bed, where she lay.

This arrangement was not good for his plan. Or for his sanity or any plan for sleep.

She lifted the covers to urge him forward. He knelt first, then slowly lowered himself to the mattress.

Ella immediately reached for him, her smooth cool fingers skimming his chest. "I feel safe here with you."

She wasn't. And she had no idea what she was doing to him. "Rest now, Ella."

She snuggled up against him, her head under his chin. "I can hear your heart beating. I like the sound."

Her seductive musky cinnamon scent closed around him, and her satiny cool hair brushed his chest like a silken caress. Pressed against him, her breasts were full and soft. "Ella, this isn't a wise idea," he managed to groan.

"I like the way you make me feel, Nathan."

She raised her head and kissed him, and he saw stars behind his eyelids. Nathan lifted to one elbow and took control of the kiss. If she showed the least hesitation or fear, he would retreat.

She wrapped her arm around his neck.

As soon as he parted his lips, she met the deep greedy kiss, her breath catching in her throat. He wanted to give to this woman, please her. He wanted to make her his.

Chapter Ten

Ella fell into the kiss with all of her being, surprising herself...almost scaring herself. What was it about Nathan Lantry that made his kisses special, that made her want to discover more of this exciting and heart-stopping wonder?

The barriers that had guarded her emotions and her heart for as long as she could remember had tumbled and lay beyond repair. She didn't even have the desire to reconstruct them because everything about this felt so right. What had started out as her attempt to bind him to her for security's sake had quickly become a living, breathing passion meant to explore and enjoy.

"Ella," he said against her lips, and the sound of her own name filled her with joy. Where the sweet response had come from, she had no idea. He trailed his fingers across her throat to her collarbone, and she'd never known a simple touch had the ability to elicit so much feeling. Her entire body wept with the pleasure, her breasts growing taut and sensitive. He spread his hand over one through the fabric of her nightdress, and she sighed with exquisite longing.

She gave herself over to the satisfaction of reaching for him, glad to meet the hair-roughened skin of his chest, where she threaded her fingers before moving to explore his side, his firm back. He was so strong and young and vital, touching him took her breath away. The strength of his body was a sharp contrast to the gentleness of his caresses as he drew a hand over her hip to her waist.

He reached for the tiny buttons down the front of her gown, and she helped him, giving him access to press kisses down her throat, her chest, and draw maddening circles around her nipple with his hot tongue.

Ella wasn't prepared for the rush of expectation and wanting that spiraled from the center of her being outward.

Lightning flashed, momentarily illuminating the room. Thunder followed, a rumble that shook the windowpanes. Ella delved her fingers in Nathan's hair. He raised the silken fabric of her gown and trailed his lips across her abdomen and lower...lower yet, where his hot damp caresses magically transformed her from the woman she'd once been to the woman she wanted to be.

She closed her eyes against the bursts of light from outdoors only to see more at the touch of his hands and lips and tongue. Without thought or hesitation, she gave herself over to the sensations he coaxed from deep within her. Her need for him, for his adoring touches was as basic as her need for air or food, equally demanding, equally intense.

When she thought she couldn't bear the exquisite torture another second, he took her tumbling over the edge of familiarity to a place of freedom and perfect rightness and release. Harsh tremors ebbed to a gentle quaking and a sublime relaxation of her limbs. Wanting to give back to him, she reached to guide him upward and take him to her. Instead of lowering his weight onto her waiting body, he gathered the comforter and pulled it up to cover her. Stretching out alongside her, he urged her to turn away so his body cupped hers from behind. The bulk of the covers separated them.

"Nathan," she said, confused.

"Shh," he said against her ear. "Just rest now."

"But, Nathan," she tried again.

"That was far beyond the boundaries of a courtship," he told her. "But you still need time to trust me."

Trust him?

"I won't spoil what we might have by rushing you." Though his voice was soft, his words were firm. He pushed the tangled hair from her neck and face so he could kiss her jaw.

Nothing in Ella's experience had prepared her for a man like this. Tender. Giving. Concerned for her well-being and placing what he assumed was her virtue above his needs and desires.

She hadn't cried since she was small, and she wasn't

going to lose control now. She swallowed the burning sensation in her throat and squeezed her eyes shut against the prickling threat, fighting for composure.

Lying in his bed, with his arms around her, his scent enveloped her, branded her. She was his wife. Nathan Lantry's wife. He'd married her after meeting her only once, even though the impulsive decision went against everything she'd learned about him. She'd believed— because it was all she knew to believe—that she would immediately become an object for his pleasure. She would fulfill his physical needs and he would provide a home and security.

He had provided the home, and so far the security... but she was no closer to sating his physical needs. The man had a will of steel.

Ella woke to sunlight stretching across the bed and warming her where she lay snuggled in a heap of bed-clothes. The luxurious sensation felt so good, she purred and stretched, finally fluttering her eyelids open.

She was alone.

She sat up and oriented herself, coming fully awake.

The previous night came back to her with an all-encompassing tingle of warmth. She let herself remember everything that had transpired between her and her husband. Every last breathtaking moment.

She smiled. A silly, self-indulgent smile.

Wondering about the disarray of her hair, she realized she would have to head for her own room to wash

and change. What time was it and where were Nathan…
and the children? She flung back the covers and stood.
After two steps, she reached Nathan's bureau and her
gaze landed upon the framed photograph.

Sitting right on top of the bureau where she couldn't
have missed it, where Nathan saw it every time he got
up and every time he went to bed, was a photograph of
Nathan seated in front of a standing woman who wore a
wedding dress and lace veil. Ella reached for the frame,
but stopped inches away and drew back her hand. The
portrait wasn't hers to touch.

But she leaned closer and examined the delicate face
of the fair-haired bride. She wasn't what might be considered beautiful by some standards, but her lips were
turned up in a sweet smile, and she had an unrivaled
purity about her. A wholesomeness that made Ella's chest
ache. Her gown was obviously satin and well made. Her
fair hair had been fashioned in a shiny soft upswept style
beneath the beaded veil. *Deborah.*

Innocent. That was all Ella could think. This woman
had come to her husband pure and untouched. Nathan
had honored her chastity just as he believed he honored
Ella by sparing her his lovemaking.

The likeness of Nathan's first wife positioned deliberately right here where he saw it each time he came to
bed…each time he woke, disturbed her in a manner she
didn't want to examine too closely. He kept Deborah
close because he loved her still. He mourned her. If Ella
hadn't flung herself at him, attempting to seduce him at
every turn, even last night wouldn't have happened.

What she'd celebrated only hours ago now seemed as sullied as everything else about her life. As sullied as everything about who she was.

Clutching her nightdress closed at her throat, she hurried from the room.

Half an hour later, she found activity in the kitchen.

"I'm sorry I overslept," she said to Mrs. Shippen, who was rubbing a bar of soap on a child-sized shirt. Charlotte stood at the sink drying dishes, and Grace and Robby were seated at the kitchen table, playing with wooden rings and a short peg on a stand. "Good morning," she said to them. "What are you playing?"

Grace held up one of the rings, about three inches in diameter so Ella could see it.

"I've never seen that game before. How do you play?"

Grace demonstrated by tossing the ring at the peg, where it caught and looped around.

"It's called Quoit," Mrs. Shippen told her. "You've seen the outdoor version, haven't you?"

"I never have," Ella answered.

"Ewwa twy," Robby said and held out a ring.

Touched that he included her in their play, Ella took it and tossed it, but missed the peg. "I guess it takes some practice."

"It's your privilege to sleep in as late as you like, Mrs. Lantry," Mrs. Shippen told her in a low voice.

Charlotte nodded. "Have a seat. I saved a plate for you."

"That's kind of you, thank you, but I can get it myself."

She found a hot pad and took the plate from the oven. Charlotte placed a fork on the table and poured her a cup of tea.

Ella ate her breakfast while the children played their game.

When she'd finished, she added sugar to her tea and sipped it. "Mrs. Shippen?" she asked. The woman turned her attention to Ella, and she continued. "Did you see the other Mrs. Lantry when she dressed for parties and went out of an evening?"

"I did, ma'am."

"Can you tell me what appropriate dress would be for this Spring Gala event?"

"The Missus always wore one of her nice gowns with elegant jewelry and gloves. And she purchased a gift for the hostess."

"What sort of gift?"

"Candy or stationery or a sachet. Something of the like."

"I suppose I'd better shop today then. Will it be convenient for me to go out this morning?"

"I'm here to make things convenient for you, not the other way around. Let me know your plans and I'll care for the children."

Ella got up and placed her plate in the sink, where Charlotte immediately washed it. Ella stood beside her as she took a towel and dried the plate. "What else did Mrs. Lantry do?"

"She made shopping lists," Mrs. Shippen replied. "She oversaw the cleaning, kept the household budget and planned an occasional party."

"How does one know what to place on a shopping list?"

Mrs. Shippen exchanged a glance with Charlotte before opening a drawer and taking out a piece of paper. Ella read it over, absorbing the logic of the necessary items. She had no idea what it took to run a household. "I'll make these purchases today."

The woman nodded. "Very well."

Ella gathered a shawl and her reticule, then paused. She walked back to the kitchen. "How do you pay?"

"Mr. Lantry has accounts at the shops. The merchants send him a bill."

"Well, isn't that convenient?"

Mrs. Shippen gave her a quizzical look as Ella turned to tell Grace and Robby she was leaving.

Simply walking down the front stairs and making her way along the edge of the brick street gave her a sense of elation. The freedom to come and go as she pleased would never grow old.

A few blocks later, she strolled along the main street, greeted by an occasional man or woman. A shopkeeper recognized her from church and waved a hello. She got a warm feeling in her chest and smiled to herself. No one turned his back or pretended not to know her. The women didn't hold their skirts aside and whisper as she passed. Ella stood studying the storefronts, familiarizing herself with the places and goods available.

Deciding on a store, she entered. The bell over the door clanged. Women's voices carried from the side of the room, but Ella went about her business and selected a box of stationery. She neared the counter and noted a woman standing back from the others, waiting to make her purchase. She held bath talc and a package of needles. Her lowered gaze didn't raise to Ella.

"Hello," the proprietress said to Ella. "Aren't you the new Mrs. Lantry?"

"Yes."

"Pleasure to make your acquaintance, ma'am. I'm Edwina Harrison. My husband runs this store."

"How do you do?"

Another woman stepped back to open their circle to Ella. "Are you looking forward to the Spring Gala, dear?"

Ella chatted a moment, and finally Edwina reached for the box of stationery, "Is this all you'd like today?"

Ella glanced at the woman who'd been there first, but who still stood silently waiting. "She was ahead of me." She took a step back and gestured to the woman. "Go ahead."

She was older than Ella, thin, with lines at the corners of her eyes. She was dressed as respectably as anyone else in the store, but her hand was void of a wedding band. A startled look crossed her features, but still she kept her face lowered, her gaze on something on a lower shelf. She shook her head. "No, you go ahead."

"Here, I'll wrap your purchase," Edwina said to Ella. "Shall I put it on Mr. Lantry's account?"

Puzzled, Ella took another step back. "No, I insist this lady go first. She was waiting when I got here."

The woman to Ella's left said in a low tone. "Bess Duncan isn't a *lady,* Mrs. Lantry."

With a sinking feeling in her stomach, Ella turned her attention from the woman who'd spoken to the one called Bess. The humiliated woman flattened her lips, and at last she looked up. The too-familiar pain and humiliation Ella saw in the depths of her faded gray eyes struck her numb. Ella had never laid eyes on Bess before, but she knew her. She knew this woman's fear and hopelessness intimately. She recognized isolation and condemnation as longtime companions. Ella stared into her own mirror image and saw despair reflected.

With supreme dignity, Bess set the two items on the nearest counter, turned on her heel and walked from the store.

The bell tolled with a grim finality.

"Of all the nerve," one of the women said. "Marching in here as though she's fit to shop with the rest of us."

Ella set the stationery on the counter, and then impulsively picked up the talcum powder and needles Bess had left behind. "I need these, too."

Edwina looked at her curiously, but she tallied the items in a ledger, wrapped them in brown paper and handed Ella the package.

Ella didn't hear anything else the women said to each other or to her. She said thank you and hightailed it out the door and onto the street.

Standing in the midmorning sun, she peered one way

and then the other, catching sight of the thin woman walking quickly away, already a block from the store.

Ella held her skirt hem above her ankles and ran along the boardwalk. At the sound of feet pounding on the wood, the woman she followed stopped and backed up against the front of the nearest building as though she anticipated an attack. As Ella neared, Bess fastened a wary look on her.

Slowing a few feet away, Ella came to a stop. Now that she was here, she didn't know what to say. Ending up like this woman was her worst fear. She glanced aside nervously, then back. Finally, she tore the wrapper from the items to remove her stationery and then rolled the paper back around the rest. She extended the package. "These are yours."

Bess didn't reach for them. "You shouldn't be seen talkin' to me. Your friends wouldn't like it none."

"I don't care what they think. Now take these, please. I know you need them," Ella said. "Please."

Slowly Bess reached for the package. She stood clutching the bundle to her breast and stared at Ella for a long uncomfortable moment. Reaching into the small drawstring bag hanging from her forearm, she pulled out a coin and held it toward Ella.

"It's a gift," Ella said with a shake of her head.

Bess blinked, but she held Ella's gaze for a long moment. Finally, she asked, "Why?"

"Because not everyone is like them," Ella answered. Something shifted behind Bess's eyes. *Gratitude.*

The emotion was painful for Ella to see. It was obvious that no one in town had treated Bess kindly in a long time. Obvious…and wrong. Ella turned and walked away.

Chapter Eleven

Ella hadn't been this nervous on her wedding day. Back then she hadn't known how important it was to fit in and not make a poor impression for Nathan's sake. She changed her dress three times, finally satisfied with her choice. The dress she deemed appropriate had a close-fitting midsection made of deep blue velvet, and the bodice had been designed to appear as though swags of pale aqua crepe de chine crisscrossed over her bosom. A full skirt of the same fabric had an overskirt adorned with gauze roses draping to a point in the front. Another rose perched on her left shoulder.

She wore a square sapphire on a silk ribbon around her neck and matching earbobs. Sheer gloves that matched the blue velvet came up over her elbows. Over her glove on her right hand, she wore a sapphire ring. She had fastened matching roses in her curled and upswept hair.

Ready now, Ella tiptoed into the nursery. Christopher's

and Robby's eyes were closed, but Grace widened hers in admiration.

Ella tucked the covers up under her chin. "Good night, little one."

Grace slipped her hand from under the covers to touch Ella's earbob, and then gave her a shy smile.

Mrs. Shippen sat in the nearby rocker, waiting for Grace to fall asleep. She smiled and encouraged Ella to have a nice evening. Descending the stairs, Ella joined Nathan in the foyer. He studied her with what she hoped was appreciation.

"Is it inappropriate?" she asked.

He found his voice. "You are the most exquisite woman I've ever laid eyes on. No one will ever notice Phoebe's stunning flower arrangements once you've arrived."

"I want you to be proud of me."

"I am the most fortunate man in all of Wyoming," he told her. He glanced down. "I think your boot has come untied."

"Oh, beans." She leaned forward to look. "I tied them after I had my gloves on."

"Allow me." He bent to one knee in his dashing black suit and motioned for her to give him her foot.

She raised her hem and complied. The bronze kid boot extended five inches above her ankle and was open down the front, with only silk lacing holding it on her foot and leg. The smart heel was all the fashion rage when she'd ordered them. Nathan tied the sash with a secure bow and stood to offer her his arm. She unfolded the lace shawl she carried and he draped it around her shoulders.

She pointed. "There's a hostess gift on the table."

He picked up the wrapped package and tucked it under his arm. "It's only a block, so I thought we'd walk," he said. "Are you able?"

"Of course."

"Sometimes ladies' slippers have no soles, and the paving is brick all the way."

"These boots have a sturdy sole for just that reason." She was glad for the time to unwind, actually. She would enjoy the walk and the refreshing evening air. Nathan took her hand, and all she could think of was the rainy night she'd spent in his bed. She glanced upward. Not a cloud in the starry night sky.

At the Crandalls' a servant took Ella's shawl at the door and ushered them along a hall and through a wide open doorway into an enormous room already milling with guests.

"Phoebe Crandall, dear," said the woman who rushed to greet them. "This is my husband, Richard."

Richard took her hand and bent over it formally. "I heard Nathan had married a beauty, but I had no idea."

Ella smiled politely. She didn't like the way he looked at her. Not as much appreciative as leering. She withdrew her hand and took Nathan's arm, handing Phoebe the gift at the same time. "A little something for you."

"Thank you, dear." She set the package on a table behind her, and Ella noticed the pile of gifts for the first time. "Help yourself to drinks along the side over there."

Nathan led Ella farther into the room and pointed to the marble-topped liquor cabinet. "Would you like a drink?"

"Whatever you have."

He poured deep red liquid into a glass and handed it to her. Nathan had been right about flowers. Every surface and even wall sconces overflowed with fragrant colorful blooms. Ella asked Nathan about each variety and he knew most of them. She couldn't help thinking of Celeste and how pleased she'd been with the simple wildflowers Ella had picked for her.

"Hello, Ella."

She turned from a floral display to recognize Lena. "I've been wondering how you were doing. I visited Celeste this week. She's very happy with her rancher."

"How nice for her." Lena spared a thin smile, then cast a glance over her shoulder as though waiting for someone. A middle-aged gentleman joined her. He nodded at Nathan.

Nathan extended a hand. "Tom."

The two men shook.

"This is my wife, Ella. Ella, Tom Bradbury."

Ella exchanged pleasantries with the man under Lena's watchful eye. "Are you enjoying our growing town?" he asked.

"It's nice here," she replied. "I like it already."

"The theater will be finished by the end of summer,"

he told her. "We'll solicit operas and plays, and have nearly all the advantages of living East."

"The theater has been Tom's pet project," Nathan informed her.

"We're trying everything to attract more women and families," the man replied. "Do you appreciate the opera?" he asked Ella. "Lena says she enjoys it."

"I've never seen one."

Lena met Ella's gaze and held it as the men spoke.

"Will you excuse us for just a moment?" Tom asked. "I want Nathan to hear something from Leland Howard." The two men walked away.

"Looks like you've landed on your feet," Lena said once they were alone.

"Marrying Nathan, you mean? He's an admirable man," Ella replied. "Kind to his children and employees, and generous with his time and attention."

"And of course *rich*," Lena remarked.

At her dry tone, Ella glanced at her. "He's well-off, yes."

"I hope you're using all of your resources to keep that man happy," Lena said. "It would be a shame if he lost interest."

Ella didn't appreciate her remark, and she had no idea what provoked it. Lena's animosity had no basis that she knew of. They'd lived under the same roof back in Dodge, eaten dinner at the same table, but had barely exchanged a dozen words until heading West with the group. Ella sipped from her glass, and Lena moved into the crowd.

Their hostess caught Ella's eye and joined her. Phoebe raised her eyebrows. "I see you found a drink."

"The sherry is good," Ella told her.

"I take a sip or two myself now and then," Phoebe said and then leaned forward. "But I wouldn't let the other ladies see me doing it."

Ella lowered her glass. "Is it unladylike?"

Phoebe tilted her head. "Some think it's unbecoming."

"Oh." Ella looked for a spot to set her glass, and Phoebe took it from her and set it behind a potted fern. "Thank you. I've been concerned about making a mistake like that. I don't want to reflect poorly on my husband."

"You couldn't reflect poorly if you tried," Phoebe said with a sincere smile. "You're far too lovely and well mannered." She gestured to a doorway. "Would you like to see my latest project?"

Phoebe led her into a lavishly decorated room that held a piano, several upholstered chairs and an array of potted plants and artwork on wrought iron stands. Every surface was covered with fringed and lace scarves, ornate frames, small fabric boxes and cut glass bowls holding flower petals and leaves.

"This screen," she told Ella, "is what I've been working on for weeks."

The object was a hinged folding screen. Hundreds of colorful images of ladies and flowers had been affixed in a detailed collage. "I covered the chair seats over the winter."

Ella noticed the needlepoint designs Phoebe referred to, as well as pillows adorned with intricately stitched flowers. She couldn't imagine the time it had taken to do all this. "You made all of these?"

The woman nodded and drew Ella's attention to an ornament made out of shells and broken bits of blue-and-white china. "I gave several of these for Christmas gifts last year."

Ella wasn't sure what it was, but she nodded. "How unique."

"What do you work on in the evenings?" Phoebe asked.

Ella mostly busied herself with seducing her husband, but she was sure Phoebe didn't want to hear about that. "I'm barely unpacked," she replied.

"Well, of course." Phoebe gestured to the screen again. "I have scraps and pictures left if you have a glue project in mind. What do you collect?"

Ella let her gaze touch on the bowls and baskets adorning surfaces. "A little of everything, much like you."

"There you are!" Betsy Iverson came through the doorway with a swish of taffeta skirts. She stopped short and admired Phoebe's folding screen. "It's just lovely. How long has it taken you?"

"Since February." Phoebe's pride was obvious in the way she held her shoulders straight and tipped her head as though acknowledging a grand accomplishment.

Ella felt decidedly awkward and unknowledgeable about the things with which these women concerned themselves. Did Nathan expect her to be stitching chair seats and pasting pictures in every spare moment? He certainly didn't expect her to do household chores, or perform sexual favors—what else remained?

"I'm afraid I'm still very new to being a wife." Ella looked from Betsy to Phoebe. "May I defer to your wisdom and expertise to ask you a few questions?"

"Certainly," Phoebe replied. "Have a seat. Betsy, join us, please."

Ella settled herself on a chair. "What exactly are your duties in your households?"

The women were more than happy to oblige her by sharing their domestic responsibilities, which included overseeing the hired help, light cleaning, meal planning and dinner party preparations.

"The school where I grew up left me sorely unprepared," Ella told them. "I have no idea how to do these things."

"I can't imagine why a girls' academy would leave their young ladies in such a state. It shows a complete lack of foresight. You certainly must learn now that you're a wife," Betsy admonished her. "Your mission is to create a paradise of peace and purity. It's the first duty of a wife to make home the most pleasant and happiest place on earth. We consult women's journals for matters of fashion, etiquette, furnishings, needlework, motifs and table settings."

"There are guidebooks, as well," Phoebe told her. "I'll loan you mine." She gave Ella a long look. "Betsy's right. It's difficult to imagine a school for young ladies that didn't teach the accomplishments necessary for home culture. I learned needlework and carried a workbag when I was but eleven years old."

"Indeed, my education was sorely lacking," Ella replied.

"What *are* your accomplishments, dear?" Betsy asked. "China painting?"

Ella's heart sank.

"Musical talent?"

"Yes!" Ella said, jumping on the last. "I read and play music. I'll be teaching the children as soon as the new piano arrives."

The other women smiled and nodded at each other as though relieved they wouldn't have to oust an uncouth guest from their presence.

"Other than that, I studied art and history and French."

"You speak French?" Betsy asked.

Ella nodded. "Fluently."

The women shared another look.

"I dare say you'll be the only woman in Sweetwater with an accomplishment that refined," Phoebe told her. "Minnie Oliver will be *green* with envy."

"And yet," Betsy said with a serious nod, "your home must be elegantly beautified. Unsightly unadorned bareness calls a woman's character into question, and you mustn't foist that indignity upon your husband."

"Of course not," Ella agreed. She glanced around, pained now by her ignorance. "I have no idea where to start."

Betsy took a deep breath and released it. "We'll help you."

Ella gave her a grateful smile.

Phoebe gestured to the piano. "Why don't you play for us?"

She had played for the guests at Madame Fairchild's most evenings. She hadn't imagined that playing for these people would be acceptable, but the women all looked at her with expectant smiles.

Nervous jitters erupted in her chest, but she moved to the piano bench.

Chapter Twelve

Sitting, Ella opened the heavy mahogany lid away from the keyboard. Phoebe owned an extraordinary instrument. Ella experienced a trill of pleasure just looking at it, and her fingers tingled with anticipation.

The hostess arranged several sheets of music so Ella could read the fronts. She didn't recognize any, but she opened one titled "Silver Threads Among the Gold" and played. The women immediately sang along.

As the song finished and the women clapped, Ella tested a few B flat major chords, immediately recalling a concerto written by a German composer. It was as natural as breathing to flow into the piece. It had been weeks since she'd played, and immediately, she fell into the music, losing herself in the notes and the passion. It never failed to amaze her that the great composers had arranged chords and measures in such a remarkable fashion as to create breathtaking pieces.

Her first teacher had convinced Madame Fairchild that *Gabrielle* had surpassed his ability to teach her, and the woman had hired a man of Russian descent to instruct her for two whole years. The lessons and practice time had been Ella's escape, and she'd soaked up every moment as a freedom to do something she enjoyed. After that, her punishment for not following Madame Fairchild's strictest orders had been banishment from the music room.

Ella had always been obedient.

The last notes of the concerto faded away, and she took a deep breath. Collecting herself, she pressed her hands together and looked up.

Betsy had tears in her eyes. The other women appeared decidedly moved, as well. Clustered around them now were the rest of the party guests, who'd gathered unbeknownst to Ella as she played. Embarrassed by the attention, she blushed and found Nathan watching her with an astonished expression.

One or two at a time, the bystanders applauded, until everyone was clapping and nodding and giving her appreciative smiles.

"That was beautiful," Mildred told her, and others agreed.

Blushing, Ella stood and made her way to Nathan. "I'd like a cup of punch."

He led her to the other room and dipped a cup of cold liquid. "I had no idea you were so gifted."

She thanked him and accepted the cup. "I told you I could play and teach."

"But I had no idea," he said again. "Many women play the piano, Ella. You are accomplished. I can't even tell you how your music made me feel. As Mrs. Evans said, it was beautiful."

For the first time, he'd truly seen her. Satisfaction flooded her being in a warm rush. She blinked hard to dispel the unaccustomed sting of tears. His appreciation for her musical ability meant more than a thousand compliments on her appearance. She was pleased to have made a positive impression on his friends, but Nathan's high regard was all that actually mattered.

She drank punch and ate a few hors d'oeuvres, but the rest of the evening was a blur because of the emotion that had risen to the surface and now colored her every movement and thought.

During the walk home, Nathan entwined his fingers with hers and later kissed her tenderly as they stood in the dimly lit foyer. She'd only ever dreamed of a man looking at her the way Nathan did, with admiration and respect. She didn't deserve either, but she wanted his esteem more than anything. For the first time she resented the necessity of her deception. She had no choice, however. She'd made a plan and followed it through, and without the lie, none of this would be hers. She had to live with the fabrication now. Somehow the ruse had to become her reality.

"Good night, Ella," her husband said in a low voice and led her up the stairs. "Sleep well."

Later, Ella couldn't fall asleep for all the ideas and concerns whirling in her head. She got up, donned her silk robe and house slippers and lit lamps in the foyer and the parlor.

The surfaces were indeed bare of ornamentation, and there was nary a scrap of lace or a tassel in sight. She would soon be expected to entertain, and this home had to reflect good taste and refinement. It was imperative she create an atmosphere to reflect positively on her husband. What she chose to do now could have an impact on his nomination and election. She would not be a detriment.

Picking up one of the women's journals that Phoebe had sent home with her, she skimmed pages, pausing to read advice that confirmed what she'd been told. "Woman should develop her artistic nature and give herself full scope in home adornment," an expert advised. The items wives created were important symbols of domesticity and feminine nature.

"A woman occupied with sewing," she read aloud, "while paying a call or sitting in front of the evening fire, presents a more captivating sight with her hands occupied by a bit of handiwork."

Nathan would find her more captivating if she held a needle and thread. Ella closed the magazine and placed it on the divan beside her. Of course, a decent man expected a chaste and moral woman, one knowledgeable about homemaking and entertaining.

She wished it were morning, so she could go to town and get her arduous task underway. She was going to make herself appealing to Nathan if it took every bit of fortitude she possessed.

* * *

During the following week, Ella purchased supplies and ordered from the catalogs at the general store. Now, rather than ordering shoes and stockings and clothing, she ordered fringe scarves and lace, as well as small boxes and a folding screen to decorate. She set up a table at one end of Nathan's study, and in the evenings, she worked on her various projects.

On Thursday she attended the choir rehearsal at church, and the other women welcomed her into their midst. One of the other girls who'd traveled to Sweetwater with their group attended, as well. Afterward when they met at Minnie Oliver's for tea, Ella recognized Rita Thomas's struggle to fit in.

Rita watched the others for her cues on how to prepare her tea and hold her china plate and cup. The poor girl's hand trembled so harshly, tea sloshed over the rim of her cup and saucer and splashed on the arm of the chair.

Minnie went for a cloth and cleaning solvent, and Rita got tears in her eyes and set down her cup.

"It's all right, dear," Minnie told her. "No harm done, see?"

Rita nodded, but she excused herself and headed for the door.

The other women blinked in distress. Betsy looked to Ella. "I don't mind talking to her, but perhaps since she's your friend, you will be more of a comfort."

Ella had only exchanged a handful of words with Rita before their trip to Wyoming, but she got up and made her way out to the porch.

Rita sat on a padded wicker chair, her hands twisted in her lap. She looked up with tears in her eyes as Ella approached. "I ruin everything I attempt."

"The chair is fine. Anyone could have spilled a little tea."

"You wouldn't have."

"Minnie feels badly that you're upset."

"I'm so nervous around these women," she admitted. "I feel like a fraud every time they look at me or talk to me."

"You're not a fraud, Rita. You're a respectable woman now. You belong here."

Rita raised luminous brown eyes. "Do you feel as though you belong?"

"I'm determined to do whatever it takes to belong," she replied. "This life is everything we ever wanted. And now it's ours. Is your new husband a good man?"

Rita nodded and relaxed her features. "Yes. He's a very good man."

"Can you be happy with him?"

She gave Ella a watery smile. "Yes."

Ella nodded. "Afternoon tea isn't such a difficult task compared to Dodge, is it?"

"Not at all." Rita took a handkerchief from her pocket and dried her eyes. "I just get so nervous around decent ladies. I feel like they can see right through me."

"Well, they can't. Put on your best smile and let's have tea." Ella got to her feet.

Rita linked her arm through Ella's and they went back inside.

Minnie's house was as effusively decorated as the Crandalls'. The walls and even the ceiling were papered with coordinating patterns and the drapes were held open with tasseled cords. Minnie displayed glass bottles and small portraits in oval frames on tables. She had a cabinet overflowing with heavy crystal stemware, and painted china plates hung in pleasing arrangements on the walls.

Ella studied the massive mantelpiece made of mirror and shelves that held china figurines. She hadn't collected *near* enough bric-a-brac yet. "Rita, will you join me in a trip to the general store this afternoon?"

"Of course," Rita replied, but she appeared surprised at the invitation.

Later, as they walked toward the main street, Ella asked, "Do you collect anything?"

"Like what?"

"I don't know. Have you seen the rooms full of things that these women own? I've studied, and a woman is expected to have all that. Anything less is uncouth."

After first stopping at the bank, where Ella had set up an account upon her arrival, they visited three stores, making purchases and placing orders. When Rita hedged that she wasn't comfortable spending her husband's money on frippery, Ella asked her if she would mind spending Ansel Murdock's money. Rita laughed and Ella paid for their purchases.

She arrived home to discover the piano had been delivered. To her amazement, it wasn't an upright version, but a lovely black lacquered baby grand. It would be another day before someone came to tune it, so for now, she admired it and planned how she would arrange and decorate the room around it.

The following day, she made a trip back downtown to purchase tables and cabinets from the furniture maker. That night she asked Nathan if she could hire someone to help her rearrange furniture, and he agreed.

Nathan had no idea what had set his new wife to this project of redecorating their home, but if it made her happy, he was glad to see her at it. On Tuesday he entered the dining room for supper to discover a piece of furniture he didn't recognize. An enormous mirror backed a massive sideboard with shelves down each side and across the top. Unfamiliar pieces of china and porcelain shone in the gaslight.

"Where did you acquire all of those dishes?" he asked as they ate supper.

"I ordered them. Do you like them?"

"Yes. Yes, I do."

Two brass vases filled with dried grass stalks and tall peacock feathers sat on either side of the mirror. "The vases are unusual."

"I bought a pair of blue-and-white porcelain vases, too, and I can't make up my mind which I like more in here, these or the others. Tomorrow I'll set out the others, so you can compare."

Nathan glanced at Mrs. Shippen, and she met his eyes, but simply ate her supper without comment. He decided to do the same.

A few days later, he arrived home from work just

as two young men were leaving. They greeted him politely and mopped sweat from their brows as they hurried down the stairs away from the house.

"Papa! Come look!" Christopher called from the far end of the entry hall.

Nathan hung his jacket on the newel post and hurried forward. The first thing he noticed was the fringed drapery hung across the doorway and fastened back to one side. The room that had been the sitting room had been transformed until he didn't recognize it. The piano took up one corner, the area behind it filled with tall potted ferns on brass stands.

The furniture was grouped into small conversation areas, and half a dozen tables and new chairs had been added.

In the center of the room stood a round dark wood table with a base that resembled a harp. Several squat pedestals holding plaster busts topped the table. Two of the men he recognized as Chopin and Beethoven, and he assumed the others were composers, as well.

Wine-colored drapes swagged to each side of the windows, revealing panels of lace curtains. Every surface held collections of shells and ornate boxes. Grace stood transfixed watching a pair of china dancers spin inside an open music box.

His first inclination was to ask where it had all come from, but words escaped him, and his loss was probably for the best.

Ella straightened from showing Robby a bowl of

marbles and approached Nathan with an expectant expression. "What do you think?"

"I—I hardly know what to think," he replied truthfully, gathering his thoughts. "It's so different."

"I wanted to surprise you."

She appeared so pleased with herself, and the attitude lit her lovely features and made her eyes twinkle. She was the most beautiful creature he'd ever set eyes on, and her smile could banish the clouds from a stormy sky. "I'm very surprised."

He walked around the room, surveying each addition, and the obvious thought and expense that had gone into the furnishing and decorating. "You do have a flair," he told her. He recognized the influence of their friends and neighbors. "I like it better than the Crandalls'."

"You do?" In a spontaneous gesture, she leaned into him and titled her face upward.

He placed the backs of his fingers against her jaw and smiled down at her. "Yes, much better."

She stood on tiptoes and he bent to give her a brief kiss. Back on her heels, she glanced at the children. "Let's wash for supper, little ones."

Grace took her hand, and Christopher followed her from the room. Robby raised both arms and chirped, "Up!"

Nathan swept him up and kissed his cheek. "What do you suppose we're having for supper, little man?"

"Chicken."

Nathan laughed and gave him a squeeze. All meat was chicken to Robby.

That evening after the children were tucked into bed, Nathan sat in his chair and observed Ella working on her folding screen project. "Where will that go?"

"The sitting room," she replied.

As if one more thing would fit. He kept the thought to himself, as well as the fact that he owned a furniture store, and had checked today, learning nothing she'd purchased had come from there. He didn't mind giving business to the other companies in town, though those owners probably thought it was odd that his wife had shopped in their stores. He'd never thought to tell her or mention it, so how could she have known? "I like all of the roses. And the cutouts of the ladies are colorful."

She wiped her fingers on a wet towel before applying another cutout to the collage. He much preferred their conversations and sitting beside her on the divan to her recent fascination with cutting and gluing, but all he really wanted was for her to be content, so he picked up his book and attempted to read.

"Do you suppose we could take the children on an outing this weekend?" she asked.

Glad for the diversion, he laid down the book. "What sort of outing?"

"Well. I read there will be jugglers and acrobats performing near Smithville. That's not far, is it?"

"About a two-hour ride. You want to see jugglers?"

"I've never seen a juggler, but I was thinking that the children would enjoy it."

"Did you read about this event in the newspaper?"

"Yes."

He skimmed news like that while searching for items of political interest. He was always looking for ways to improve the city and to make the territory safer for his family and others. He most often thought about his children's futures and educations, not ways to entertain them. But the light in her eyes and the lift in her voice suggested they needed to have fun, as well. He appreciated that she was the perfect foil to his blind ambition.

"We'll leave early Saturday then," he said.

Her smile touched him. Made him want to get up, cross the room and kiss her until she melted and they were both trembling as they had been the night of the thunderstorm.

Nathan thought of that experience at least a hundred times a day and at the most inappropriate times. She was his wife, and she had never shown the least resistance or distaste regarding his advances. Her acceptance made his self-imposed restraint all the more difficult.

He was certain that if he did go to her now, she wouldn't resist. He imagined crossing the room and urging her from her seat and into his arms. He remembered the feel of her hair in his hands and against his skin...couldn't forget her intoxicating scent or the feel of her warm and willing body.

He'd set an impossible restriction when he'd chosen to court Ella for six months before making love to her. He hadn't counted on wanting her so badly. He'd done the right things for the right reasons, he assured himself now. Just because waiting was difficult didn't mean he'd made a poor decision.

He was a man of character and discipline. He rigidly adhered to what was right and he learned from his mistakes. Doing what was right was more important than slaking his physical needs.

Ella wiped her hands and glanced at the clock before standing and moving toward him. Spiraling need made him achingly uncomfortable, and at her approach desire for her quickened.

She knelt in front of him and rested her hand on his knee. "I'm looking forward to Saturday. Thank you."

"Don't thank me," he said gruffly, but he leaned toward her and reached for her shoulders to urge her closer.

Chapter Thirteen

She complied, rising to meet his lips. He intended to keep the kiss casual, but as soon as his lips touched her warm soft ones, he slanted his head and invited a deeper, more intimate contact, loving her sleek heated textures and the way she made a little sigh of pleasure deep in her throat.

She wasn't put off by his kiss, nor did she show any sign of pulling away or slowing him down. Kissing her was risky business because she seemed to like it as much as he did. One of them needed to come to his or her senses before he did exactly what he dreamed of doing and took her up to his bedroom.

He drew away. He touched the wisp of hair at her cheek and gazed into her bright shining eyes, still so filled with wonder and appreciation. He never wanted to see that look change. He never wanted to disappoint her.

He found his voice. "It's late. We'd better get some rest."

Ella disguised her unladylike disappointment and tidied up her project and supplies. For the first time, self-doubt flickered through her thoughts. The unfinished sealing of their vows had become a worry. Was there something about her that made it *easy* for Nathan to delay consummating their marriage?

Ella could hardly sleep Friday night. Nathan had thought it best they didn't tell the children about the trip, lest they become overexcited. If her own anticipation was any indication, he'd been right.

He'd given Mrs. Shippen Saturday off. Charlotte prepared breakfast and packed sandwiches and apples for their journey, then left.

Nathan loaded their belongings into the buggy and they gathered the children. Robby was the most excited, pointing and calling out about cows and horses in pastures as they passed.

"What's a acrobat, Papa?" Christopher asked.

"Men and women swing from a bar high above the ground and perform tricks."

"Have you ever heard the acrobat song?" Ella asked.

Christopher answered that he had not.

"He'd fly through the air with the greatest of ease," she sang and Nathan joined her. *"That daring young man on the flying trapeze."*

They continued and, because she'd played the song several times and knew the words by heart, she supplied them. When the song ended, Robby and Grace clapped.

Nathan looked over to catch sight of Ella laughing with them over her shoulder. His chest dipped with affection for this young woman and her appreciation for every small nuance of life. He'd been so preoccupied with work and his plans for an election that it had been too long since he'd taken time to enjoy small moments such as these.

Deborah had never shown this much appreciation for anything he'd tried to do to cheer her up or make her content. When had he stopped trying and turned his focus to his career? He was ashamed for not planning enjoyable activities for his children.

Reaching over, Nathan captured Ella's hand in his large strong grasp. Never had she felt so safe or so bursting with simple happiness. She turned a deliberately shining smile toward him to show him her pleasure.

"I'm grateful you suggested this," he told her.

"I'm glad to be here," she replied.

The look on his face showed his surprise at her words.

During the ride Robby fell asleep, and Nathan woke him when they arrived in Smithville. The event had drawn vendors and spectators from the surrounding area. Makeshift booths lined the central dirt street, and colorful handbills had been tacked to every post and fence and doorway in sight. Nathan plucked off a paper and handed it to Christopher. "It's a drawing of the acrobat."

Christopher stared with wide-eyed fascination. "Can I keep it?"

"Of course you may," his father replied.

Grinning, the boy folded the paper clumsily and stuck it into his pocket.

The first acrobatic performance didn't start for another hour, so they strolled past booths that offered everything from candy and wooden toys to photography and souvenirs.

They paused and Nathan studied a tent with a sign thrust into the dirt outside. He turned to her. "Shall we have a photograph taken?"

Immediately she thought of the portrait of himself and his wife that sat atop his bureau. "If you wish."

He nodded and urged his family toward the tent. Inside, several handsome photographs were displayed in frames on easels in front of a long narrow table. Behind the display a piece of canvas divided the rest of the tent into privacy. A man in a gray suit and red tie came out from behind the temporary wall.

"What a handsome family," he remarked. "Would you like several photographs for family members? Perhaps one for each of the children so they will own heirlooms."

"Is that possible?" Nathan asked.

"Indeed," the photographer said. "I'm using glass negatives and the collodion wet plate, so I can develop clear and detailed portraits. I can make several from the same negative."

"One for us and one for each of the children, then," Nathan decided.

Ella touched his arm. "You should have a portrait taken alone for the campaign."

Nathan raised his eyebrows at her forethought. "Excellent idea."

Ella located the small ivory comb she kept in her bag and prepared the children's hair. Nathan asked to borrow it, and then they posed, taking turns with one adult sitting on a curved parlor chair while the other stood with the children. When Nathan was seated, he held Robby on his lap and the other family members circled him.

Once they'd finished, the photographer took Nathan's money and told him what time to come back for the finished portraits.

Back in the sunshine, the area was a noisy and colorful mishmash of tents and vendors. The aromas of beer, boiling sausages and cinnamon buns blended into sensory overload.

A juggler in a red tuxedo costume tossed six or eight balls into the air and caught one at a time, immediately sending it back into the rotation. Robby watched, transfixed.

A man on stilts walked past, catching the children's attention. Passing a booth, the mouthwatering smells of caramel and popcorn waylaid them next. Nathan bought them each a popcorn ball, and one for Ella. She tasted it and her eyes widened. "This is so good. Can we make these at home?"

He laughed. "I imagine so. My mother used to do it. Corn syrup and butter hold them together."

Eventually they took seats on wooden stands that lined a bare area where mattresses had been piled under a framework of poles and wires with single bar swings swaying high above the ground.

Grace leaned against her father and pointed to her crossed legs. He lifted his gaze to Ella's. "She has to use the necessary."

Ella handed Nathan her reticule and the last half of her popcorn ball. "I'll take her."

By the time she and Grace returned, the benches were filled with spectators and a band had begun to play a lively number. Nathan got out his handkerchief and wiped sticky hands and faces.

At the appointed time, a man in a tuxedo and top hat came out into the open area. Through a megaphone, he introduced the dangerous and death-defying duo of Hubert Stratton and Little Lou Beatty, the high-flying artists of the trapeze.

The crowd applauded and shouted to welcome the man and woman dressed in what appeared like ornately embellished Shakespearean garb from the torso up. Below their waists they wore brief diaperlike pants and snug stockings.

To loud cheers, the two immediately climbed rope ladders on opposite sides of the arena. Once at the top, they situated themselves on the bar swings and began pendulous motions in opposition to each other.

The performers swung high above the ground, and the very real danger of falling soon quieted the crowd. Next the man and woman stood on their swaying bars and waved to the people. Christopher and Robby waved and squealed in return. Grace widened her eyes, and her mouth formed an O as the acrobats wrapped their legs around the bar and swung upside down. The crowd oohed and ahhed in amazement.

Nathan enjoyed watching the children and Ella as much or more than he appreciated the performance. Ella's rapt expression revealed her enchantment. She glanced at him once, caught him watching her and smiled shyly. "Isn't it exciting?"

"It is," he agreed.

Once Hubert and Little Lou took to swinging out until one could let go and fly over to be caught by the other, the crowd drew a collective breath and then released it each time neither performer fell. The electrifying elements of anticipation and danger held each spectator mesmerized. It wasn't long before Nathan, too, watched and became caught up in the excitement.

The crowd cheered and gasped and applauded at the appropriate times, and when the acrobats climbed down and their feet touched the ground, the children seemed disappointed. Their unhappiness didn't last long, however, because clowns and men on unicycles replaced the acrobats as the center of attention.

Eventually, the performances ended, and the Lantrys once again walked the rows of vendors and salesmen.

Nathan paused at a booth selling photographs of the performers. The sepia-toned likenesses were mounted on heavy card stock and an array of stands and albums could be purchased to hold them. He asked each of the children to select one, and he paid for them.

Eventually, they picked up their family portraits and found a busy restaurant where they ate before heading for home. Robby and Grace fell asleep on the rear seat, and Ella invited Christopher to join them in the front, where he had more room without heads and legs lying atop his lap and could better enjoy the scenery. He gave her a grateful smile and situated himself between her and Nathan.

"It sure was a fun day, Papa."

"It was Ella's idea, actually. She's the one who suggested we go."

"Thank you." He gave her another tired grin. "This was the best day ever. I'm glad you came to marry us and be in our family."

His unexpected comment caused Ella's throat to seize up.

She glanced up at Nathan, finding him gauging her reaction, and then dropped her gaze right back to the boy. She swallowed and tested her voice. "It—it means a lot to me that you said so, Christopher. I'm very glad I married your father and joined your family, too. I never had a family before this one, so I'm still learning."

"You didn't have no family at all? None?"

She shook her head to affirm she had none.

"Did your mama die, too?"

"Yes. She did."

"What about your papa? Didn't he take care of you when your mama died?"

"He died, too."

"Oh." He looked from her up to his father and slid his hand along his father's trouser leg, until Nathan reached down and enfolded the child's fingers into his much larger hand.

Eventually, even Christopher wore out and leaned heavily against her shoulder. She raised her arm to hold him more closely, and he curled against her and slept soundly. She threaded his wavy fair hair away from his temples and studied his profile. Glancing up, she discovered Nathan watching her, but he looked away.

Once at home, they woke the children, and she ushered them inside to eat a sandwich, then wash and change for bed while Nathan returned the horses to the livery.

Once the young ones were all tucked into bed, she heated water for a bath and closed herself in the chamber behind the kitchen.

A light tap sounded on the door. "Save the water for me," Nathan called. "I'll use it and dump the tub."

She finished and then dressed in her nightclothes and wrapper and entered the empty kitchen to make a pot of tea. After enjoying two cups, she rinsed the cup and wandered out to find the package Nathan had rested on a tabletop in the foyer.

One of the portraits of the family was larger than all

the rest, and Nathan had bought a frame which now held it. In the photograph, he stood behind Ella as she sat on the parlor chair with the children around her. She studied the portrait, noting the satisfaction in her own expression and the pride in Nathan's. She carried the frame to the sitting room and found a prominent spot on the piano, then changed her mind and moved it to a table.

Studying it reminded her of Nathan's photograph of his wife. This photograph was deceptive. If a stranger looked at it he would imagine she belonged here and that she was the mother of these children. She wasn't, of course. She was someone who'd come along later and filled a space in the family group. But maybe, just maybe, if she tried hard enough, the feeling of being alone and unwanted would fade.

Turning away, she spotted the piano. She'd barely had any time to touch the beautiful instrument since it had been tuned, so she sat on the bench, opened the lid and played a few scales. The resonating deep tones sent a tingle up her spine.

She had sheet music in a trunk upstairs, but she'd learned many compositions by heart. One particular piece came to her, and she played the opening measures. More came to mind, and she let the music sweep her away as it so often did.

Most often, playing was an escape from her ordinary world, her only opportunity to lose herself and forget who she was and what she did. Tonight however, she had no desire to forget this day or the family with whom she lived or to lose part of herself. She played for the sheer beauty of the moment, pouring her feelings of gratitude and joy into the notes.

After finding himself something to eat, Nathan left the kitchen and sought out Ella where she sat at her piano. She created a stark contrast, delicate and feminine in shimmery white against the massive black instrument. He couldn't have said which was more captivating: the sight of her enraptured by the chords and the flow of notes or the amazing sounds she produced with her delicate wrists and slender fingers coaxing magic from the ivory keys. Her appearance was angelic, her playing a heavenly sound.

Watching her, he experienced a recurring thought: everything about her was perfect. She got along well with his children. She blended into their family and their household. His nanny and cook liked her, and she liked them. A cross word never left her lips, and she was appreciative of even the smallest thing.

Of all the men who'd shown up to propose, how had he been so fortunate as to have her say yes? What great hand of fate had rested upon him with favor that day?

His good fortune was overwhelming.

The last notes faded away and Ella drew her hands from the keys to rest flat on either side of her hips on the mahogany bench.

"I've never heard anything so beautiful," he said.

"Oh!" She turned, surprise registering. "I didn't know you were there."

"I didn't mean to startle you. You were pretty involved in that piece of music."

She shifted her knees around the bench, bringing to his attention her bare feet beneath the hem of her night-dress. Noticing his look, she tucked her toes back under the fabric. "I hope I didn't disturb you."

"Quite the contrary. I enjoy your playing very much."

"I plan to start lessons on Monday." She got up and turned back to close the lid over the keyboard. "I was thinking."

"About what?"

"That I could give lessons to other children and add to the household income."

Her suggestion caught him by surprise, as did nearly everything about her. Did she have the idea that he was unable to provide for them adequately? "It's a facet we've never discussed, these financial matters. But I've certainly never said anything about your shopping or expenditures that would make you think we have a need. I earn an adequate sum, Ella."

"I'm sorry I brought it up." Turning away, she looked at the photograph where it stood on the round center table between Bach and Mozart. With a hesitant gesture, she indicated the composers and the table. "I purchased these things and the furniture with my own money."

Nathan absorbed that fact with more than a little trouble. "I...I just assumed you put your purchases on the accounts at the stores. I own a couple of those businesses, you know. I acquire stock at wholesale."

"They gave me wholesale prices," she replied. "But I figured out the totals ahead of time, withdrew funds and paid cash."

Where had she come by that much money, and why had she spent it on furnishings? "Why?"

Chapter Fourteen

~~~

She faced him again and met his eyes with a cautious glance. "I wanted to bring something to our marriage."

Her words left an ache in his chest. She'd already brought so much. How could she think differently?

"I never intended to insult your ability as a provider or head of the household."

"You didn't insult me, Ella," he said finally. "You humble me." He took a few steps toward her, and she immediately met him and pressed into his embrace, her cheek against the front of his shirt. Her shoulders were slim and delicate, and her damp hair smelled fresh and uniquely spicy. Through the fabric of their clothing, her soft breasts crushed against his chest.

Glancing over her shoulder, he spotted their portrait. The image of them together touched him. He tangled his fingers into her cool and silky damp hair and caressed her scalp.

"I never knew a family would be like this." She hadn't meant for her voice to sound so husky or full of emotion. "I had no idea that I'd feel the way I do about having a husband."

He bracketed her shoulders and held her away so he could see her face. "And how *do* you feel about having a husband?"

"Proud," she replied quickly. Then with a smile added, "Confused." Her smile faded. "And so frightened that I'll make a mistake."

"Everybody makes mistakes." He rested the backs of his fingers against her jaw.

"And to be perfectly honest," she added. "I feel as though you're holding me at arm's length, so that if I make too big of a mistake you can still change your mind about me."

Her revelation gave him pause. "Because of my courtship rule?"

Her regret over admitting her lack of confidence was immediately recognizable in the way she averted her gaze and stiffened in his arms. She backed away.

He caught her hand and didn't let her go far. "You know why I set that date."

"I know you think it's logical and necessary, and I respect your wisdom to make the choice." That glimmer of vulnerability was gone, and she gave him a smile. "It's late, and we have church in the morning."

Withdrawing her hand from his, she turned and left the room.

When only her scent and the beguiling taste of her on his lips remained, he turned down the wicks in the lamps. He had a bad feeling that his hesitation was serving only to drive her away, and that was the last thing he wanted. He needed to rethink his plan. He couldn't lose her.

The following week, Ella introduced each of the children to the piano. Robby was the biggest challenge, but she chose to instruct him on his own level, regardless.

At choir rehearsal, she learned that Lena and Tom Bradbury had taken a trip to Cheyenne, where they'd been married.

"I wonder why they didn't get married in Sweetwater and invite us," Mildred mused aloud.

Minnie served tea and passed the tray of lemon cakes. "If you ask me, she was in a hurry to tie the knot and didn't want any interference."

"What do you mean?" Betsy asked.

"I invited her to tea," Minnie said. "And she turned up her nose like there was a bad smell in the room."

"She hasn't attended church anywhere," Betsy added. She glanced around sheepishly. "I checked the other denominations."

"I hope Tom knows what he's doing," Phoebe Crandall added. "He's a good man."

The others nodded and clucked as though worried he'd joined himself to a problem wife.

All along, Lena's animosity had surprised Ella, but she wished the best for her. Not everyone escaped the life they'd once led unscathed.

As that week moved into the next, Nathan and Ella accepted two more invitations and attended dinner parties. One evening, Ella spoke to Nathan about hosting their own. "I think the house is ready," she told him. "The furnishings and decor will reflect well on you. I've been doing a lot of reading on the topic, and a candidate running for an office as important as governor should be building social relationships and showing the voters that his family looks up to him and that his morals are above reproach."

Nathan smiled at what seemed like her earnest desire to make a place for herself in their home and the community.

"There is an intricate linkage between design and behavior," she continued. "And when society recognizes your irreproachable good taste, they will trust you."

"All they need do is see *you* to recognize my good taste," he teased and stole a kiss.

"I am completely serious."

He raised her hand to his lips and kissed her fingers. "I know. And I find it charming."

"We will select a date and I'll send invitations, then."

With a pleasure he couldn't have anticipated, he agreed. His first wife had never gone to such lengths to create an atmosphere in hopes of pleasing him or impressing his peers. Of course, Sweetwater had changed and grown even further since her death, so he couldn't be entirely critical.

But even taking the changes into consideration, he couldn't imagine that Deborah would have worked as diligently as Ella had to see that their home reflected favorably upon him. Ella had a determination and strength about her Deborah had never exhibited.

The following Friday evening they attended a dinner at Carl and Athena Lawrence's. Ella had only met the couple once or twice. They were older than most of the other pairs, and Athena spoke often of Carl selling the mill he owned so they could move back East.

"I still have a sister in upstate New York," she told Ella and Minnie. "I'd like to spend some time with her and once again enjoy city life before I die of old age and boredom here."

"Oh, Athena, you're forever speaking of New York as though it's the be-all and end-all of civilized existence," her husband chided.

"Because it is." She clearly wasn't amused.

Ella glanced up and caught Nathan's eye, recognizing his empathy for his friend. It was obvious that Carl had lived his life here in Sweetwater with a discontented wife who didn't hesitate to make her displeasure known. Ella studied Athena, trying to comprehend her reasoning and sympathize with her misery. Ella didn't know the story or the pain behind the woman's desire to live elsewhere. She didn't want to judge her, but it was difficult to understand how life here could be considered a hardship by any means.

But life was subjective, as were people's feelings and reactions, and she admonished herself to remember that.

Tom and Lena had returned from their trip to Cheyenne, and the newlyweds were the center of attention as Tom shared the story of their decision to marry.

Lena described the hotel where they'd stayed. "The food served in the dining room was incredible. Even the locals ate there. We need a hotel just as lavish here in Sweetwater," she told the nearby guests.

A maid spoke to Athena and their hostess announced dinner. Nathan caught Ella's hand as she joined the guests headed for the dining room.

"I've been thinking of something," she said to him.

"What is it?"

"Celeste and Paul aren't invited to these events. Would it be inappropriate for us to include them when we have our dinner parties?"

"It's our home, and she's your friend. You may invite whomever it pleases you to invite."

"Thank you, Nathan."

He tugged her away from the others and guided her into an alcove. "Thank *you*," he said to her.

"For what?"

"For every day," he answered.

Puzzled, she frowned.

"For being content and for working so hard at making the children happy."

"I am content, and children deserve happiness. It takes very little to please them, actually."

"As it does you," Nathan said.

She didn't understand entirely, but she knew he'd been affected by listening to their hostess. "Nathan," she said, "what you've given me is not a small measure. I could never begin to tell you, but..." She held back unfamiliar emotion that threatened to well up in an embarrassing and revealing display. She couldn't finish the sentence, and didn't even know what she was going to say.

Reaching for her, Nathan swept her close and held her gently against him, careful not to muss her beaded evening gown or her hair. She inhaled his scent of starch and soap and raised a hand to his jaw.

He kissed her with a sweet, almost desperate passion that left her breathless and light-headed. When he released her, she steadied herself by grasping his arm.

"Let's go to dinner, Mrs. Lantry."

He turned and she changed her hold to slip her arm through the crook of his and let him lead her back to the dining room. The other guests had already been seated. Athena gave Ella a knowing smile and gestured for them to take their places.

The past couple of weeks, Nathan had given a lot of thought to Ella's words. She'd told him she felt he was holding her at arm's length. She had quickly covered up hurt she didn't want him to see, but the more he thought about it, the more he knew she was still uneasy about their relationship.

Lately, when he thought about it, he'd known she was right. If he didn't let her too close, she couldn't reject him or his home or what he stood for.

His constant comparisons to Deborah had only reinforced what he'd glimpsed from the very beginning. Ella was nothing like his first wife. He warned himself every day and chose to keep Deborah's discontent foremost in his mind in all of his interactions with Ella. Holding his new wife to those standards had become decidedly difficult.

And unfair.

His need to be in control had become a safety measure devised to keep from disappointing her and therefore losing her. If he didn't let her down, things should go on as they were.

He barely tasted Athena's savory beef or the tender vegetables in Hollandaise sauce. His attention remained on Ella. She visited with James Evans on her other side, occasionally answering his wife Mildred's questions about French words.

Ella took a few bites and lifted her gaze to Nathan's. "Do you like asparagus?"

"Yes."

"You haven't touched yours."

He looked down and sliced a spear with the silver knife and fork.

Dinner took forever, and when it was finished, Nathan joined the men in Carl's study for an obligatory glass of brandy. Carl offered cigars and a few of the others accepted.

When at last Carl suggested they join their wives, Nathan was the first one through the doorway.

"Perhaps Ella will play something for us," Phoebe suggested, gesturing to Athena's lace-draped harpsichord.

"Unfortunately, we need to get back to the children," Nathan replied immediately. "Mrs. Shippen can't stay late this evening."

"I'm dreadfully disappointed," Athena said. "I haven't heard you play yet, but I hear you are extremely gifted."

"You'll all be receiving invitations to our home soon," Ella told her and glanced at the others. "I'll be glad to play something for you then. Mr. Lantry has purchased an exquisite piano. I've never played such a fine instrument."

The Olivers and the Iversons wished them a good night, and Athena handed Nathan his hat and Ella her shawl.

"Thank you for the delicious meal," Ella told her. "I only hope I can do half as well planning a menu."

"I'm sure you will, but if you should need any help, don't hesitate to call on me."

Out of doors, Nathan took her hand as they walked along the brick street.

"Mrs. Shippen can't stay late this evening?" Ella asked. "I thought she was spending the night in the downstairs bedroom."

"I wanted to leave."

"Oh." She looked away. Her heels clicked on the paving bricks. She glanced up at him. "Are you feeling ill?"

"I'm perfectly well, thank you."

She didn't recognize his abrupt mood, so she held her tongue and enjoyed the cool evening air and the sky full of stars. There wasn't a cloud visible, and the heavens twinkled as though they were filled with multifaceted diamonds.

Ella thought of Grace's delight at hearing her play "The Star" and smiled. Spontaneously, she sang softly, *"When the blazing sun is gone, when he nothing shines upon; then you show your little light, twinkle, twinkle, all the night."* She hummed it through again. "Some experts believe that Wolfgang Mozart wrote that song, did you know that?"

"I didn't."

"The original version was French, of course, but several versions have been arranged from that first melody, including one by Mozart."

"Your pretty head is stuffed with facts about explorers and composers."

Was he having fun with her now? She looked at him, but his smile wasn't teasing.

When they reached the house, Nathan unlocked the door and ushered her inside. "Go on upstairs. I'll bring you warm water and a glass of sherry."

She almost told him she could get her own water, but the look on his face stopped her. She gathered her hem and hurried up the stairs. Mrs. Shippen had helped her with this particular dress, as the pearl buttons were tiny and the bodice formfitting. She could only reach partway and would need help.

Plucking pins from her hair, she loosened the curls

and let them fall around her shoulders, then brushed the tresses loose.

A light tap sounded at the door, and Nathan pushed it open. He carried a pitcher behind the dressing screen, then went back out and returned with two glasses and a short square bottle on an ebony tray. He carried a half-full glass to Ella where she sat.

She studied the pale liquid before taking a sip. "This isn't as sweet. I like it better than the last."

"What do you know about sherry?" he asked.

"I know it's from Spain. May I see the bottle?"

"I'll be certain to keep a supply on hand." He handed her the bottle and she read the label.

"Only wine made from grapes grown in the Sherry Triangle can be called sherry," she told him. "The wine is fortified with brandy sometime after the fermenting process."

"Explorers, composers and wine. You had an interesting education."

She handed the bottle back and he set it on the tray.

She sipped from her glass. "When Ferdinand Magellan stocked up to sail around the world, he spent more money on sherry than he did on weapons."

"Must have been quite a trip." Smiling, Nathan stepped behind her. "Stand up and I'll get those buttons for you."

She did as he asked, and he worked them loose, inching his way down her spine until the back of the dress gaped open. "Do you know what that glass you're holding is called?"

She glanced at the tulip-shaped stemmed glass with its delicate bowl that narrowed at the top. "I don't know."

"A *copita*," he told her.

"Spanish? Where did you learn that?"

He grinned and then leaned to fill her glass again. "From the salesman in Denver who sold them to me. What kind of girls' school teaches young ladies about wine?"

"We got a very well-rounded education at Miss Haversham's."

"Obviously." He stepped close to kiss her neck. "Did they ever warn you that men might ply you with spirits and then try to seduce you?"

Chapter Fifteen

This was a side of him she'd never seen before. Playful. *Seductive.* Starting where his lips touched, a tingling shiver of delightful warmth spread across her shoulders to her breasts, and they tightened. "Of course I was warned."

She finished the rest of the liquid in her glass and set it aside so she could drape one arm around his shoulder and bring herself closer to him. "Do you think it will rain?"

He frowned in puzzlement for only a moment. "You're not afraid of storms, are you?"

She shook her head and smiled.

"I couldn't take my eyes off you this evening." He kissed her collarbone, and her eyelids fluttered closed. He inhaled against the skin at her throat, as though absorbing her essence, and touched his tongue against her neck, followed by an openmouthed kiss.

Ella feared she would melt into a puddle of sheer pleasure.

Nathan straightened. Slowly and deliberately, he grasped the fabric of her bodice and peeled it outward. She slid her arms out of the openings. Kneeling, he held her gown so she could step out of it. He straightened and draped it half over the bench, half on the floor without concern, then turned back to step behind her and search the waist of her half petticoat for the drawstring. He tugged the bow loose and inched the eyelet and lace down over her hips, not bothering to pick up the garment after she kicked it away. It lay in a stiff heap.

She couldn't have been more surprised at this turn of events or his obvious intent. Nor, if this was leading where she thought it was, could she have been more delighted. Yes, she wanted to consummate their marriage and seal herself to him, but she also craved his touches and had thought about their last amazing encounter for weeks.

Afraid to do anything that would stop him or call a halt to this moment, she rested her palms against his chest, testing his response to her touch.

He caught her hair and moved it aside, so he could gently brush his fingertips over her shoulder. He leaned in and tilted his head to kiss her. The rush of exhilaration she derived from his kiss was beyond words.

She'd never anticipated her fascination with his caresses. Until now a man's touch had been a means to an end. A job to perform to the best of her ability and without commitment or connection to the person. Her countless new surprising physical and emotional reactions were frightening, because she had everything to lose if this marriage didn't work out.

He straightened and looked at her this time, his gaze taking in her eyes, mouth and her hair as though he found her responses surprising, as well. He took a step back, separating them, and though they no longer touched, electricity crackled between them.

Daring to make a move, she reached for the buttons of his shirt and unfastened them. He lifted his hand to turn his wrist inward and remove his cuff link. The other cuff followed and he set the gold studs beside their glasses on the dressing table before turning her by one shoulder and reaching for the clasp of her necklace. "You have very nice jewelry. Gifts from admirers?"

Without replying, she turned back to part his shirt and peel the cotton away. He shrugged out of it, and his skin glowed in the lamplight. He sat on her bench to remove his shoes and stockings, then patted the seat between his thighs, indicating she should rest her foot there.

She did so, balancing herself by touching his bare shoulder as he untied the satin laces of her kid boot and removed it. Meanwhile, she appreciated the sight of his broad muscled shoulders and well-sculpted hair-dusted chest.

Running both open hands up her leg and under the hem of her pantaloons, he found her garter and unfastened her stocking. With a quick upward glance at her face, he rolled the stocking downward until he could tug it from her foot and drop it.

She shifted her weight and offered the other shoe and stocking, which he disposed of in the same slow, efficient manner. This time, he hooked a hand behind her knee, preventing her from lowering her leg, and sensuously caressed her calf. He slid his touch higher, skimming her thigh. Ella's heart sped up, and she remembered the way he'd made her feel that night she'd lain in his bed with thunder rumbling and lightning streaking the bedclothes with jagged illumination.

She caught her breath and locked her gaze with his. The dark shadows of his eyelashes drifted down once. Twice. He held her gaze, but he swallowed, and in that moment she recognized his own uncertainty. His first wife hadn't been happy with her life. Had she been unhappy with Nathan specifically—or with the physical aspect of their marriage? Ella wished she didn't know about men with unhappy wives, but the income those kind of men generated had kept their parlor house in excellent repair and provided food and clothing no one else in Kansas could afford.

Ella immediately recalled Athena Lawrence's complaints about life here in Sweetwater. Nathan had been unable to look at Carl after his wife's comments. Athena's discontent had obviously disturbed Nathan, because right after that he'd taken Ella aside. He identified with Carl Lawrence's plight because Deborah hadn't been happy, either.

Had Nathan's hesitation or his determination to extend their courtship been based on fear of taking a wife who wasn't happy with *him?*

Knowing him as she did, she didn't think he'd be like plenty of other men who sought a welcome elsewhere, claiming their wives were cold or unwilling. He'd honored his wife and his vows and lived faithfully in an unhappy marriage.

What did he have to be uncertain about now, other than his concern over displeasing her? His concern humbled her to the point of strong emotion that welled up and filled her chest with an uncomfortable, but exquisite burning sensation. She wanted to reassure him.

"I did have a few admirers back where I came from," she admitted. "But I chose to travel here. And to marry you."

His focus drifted to her hands as she brought them to the front of her corset and unfastened the hooks with little popping sounds. He continued to watch after she'd let it fall and tugged on the satin ribbon that held her chemise closed. The style she wore had no buttons, and she crossed her arms over her chest and grabbed the hem to pull it off over her head.

His eager hands were immediately there to help her.

The garment dangled from his fingers for a moment before falling onto the growing heap of discarded clothing.

The cool air that touched her breasts felt good, but after removing the constrictive corset her rib cage itched. She rubbed the tender skin that was covered with indentions, and his dark gaze followed.

"It itches?" he asked.

"Something fierce."

He replaced her hands with his rougher palms, and she expelled a sigh that turned into a purr of contentment.

The lamplight created tantalizing shadows in the hollows and swells of his muscled chest, so when he looked at her body, she imagined he had much the same reaction to the sight of her.

"You are so beau—"

She pressed her fingers against his lips. "Don't say it. Please. Don't tell me I'm beautiful."

"But you—"

"No," she said forcefully. "Beauty means nothing. *Nothing.* I can't help the way I look. I have no control over that and it says nothing about me. Tell me I've done a good job with the children or that I know more about French explorers than anyone else you know, but don't praise my appearance."

He gave her a curious glance. "What kind of woman are you?"

She shook her head and forced a hoarse reply. "Just a woman who wants to be with you tonight."

His eyes darkened with passion. He brought his hands up under her breasts, and she melted beneath his touch. With his thumb, he grazed one peak in a back-and-forth motion that made her catch her breath.

"You have the best French accent I've ever heard," he said. If he was teasing her, she didn't care.

"Have you heard many?"

"No." He leaned forward and kissed her, all the while continuing the maddening caress. "You *are* good with children, and you put people at ease as soon as they meet you."

"Really?"

"Yes. The women look a little intimidated at first, but as soon as you speak and ask questions about them, they warm right up to you."

"No, I mean about the children."

"You're a natural." He kissed her again, and she looped both arms around his neck to hug him soundly.

He folded her against him, and then tucked both hands under the twin swells of her buttocks. He spoke against her lips. "Ella, do you know what we're doing?"

"I know."

"Did they teach young ladies about the physical aspect of marriage at Miss Haversham's?"

"You can't disappoint me, Nathan. Nothing will happen that I don't want to happen. I want you. I like the way you make me feel. It's real and it's honest, and I've never felt this way before."

He urged her until the backs of her knees touched the mattress, and she fell backward onto the bed. He followed and moved his mouth to her breast.

A dizzying rush of pleasure consumed Ella, and she arched upward, her heart pounding, eager for his touch, hungry for the way he made her feel. Part of her was afraid of the feelings she'd never before experienced—had never allowed. And part of her rejoiced in the joyful freedom of holding nothing back. When his hot mouth sent shivers coursing through her, she closed her eyes and relished the sensations.

"I ache for you, Ella," he said, holding himself taut above her. "It's a need like nothing I've ever felt before, but I won't do anything that doesn't please you."

"I don't think you could do anything that doesn't please me," she answered breathlessly. "I'm pretty certain we'll both be pleased." She grasped his shoulder. "Not like last time."

"No, not like last time," he agreed. He dropped his head and nipped at her skin, kissing, nipping, making his way across her shoulder, her breast.

Ella locked her arm around his neck and forced him up to kiss her. They clung together and rolled to one side, where she worked her arm between them to unfasten his trousers and reach for him, thick and swollen.

A firestorm of emotion and sensation burst inside Nathan at her eager touch. He kissed her with all the longing and passion he'd denied himself for so long. Yes, he was impatient to make love to her, but even more eager to please her. He groaned her name against her chin...her neck...her ear....

"Do you want to prevent a child?" she asked softly.

The question caught him off guard. She was full of surprises, this woman. "How do you know about such things, Ella?"

"Well, I—I asked one of the married women a few questions."

He couldn't in a million years imagine Deborah ever doing such a thing. But Ella had wanted to come to him prepared. The gesture touched him deeply. "No," he replied. "I would welcome a child." He cleared his head enough to ask, "And you?"

She looked at him in surprise. "You're asking what I want?"

"Of course. You would be the one carrying an infant inside your body—the one giving birth and nursing a baby. You should be able to decide if you're ready for that. Or—if you ever want that."

He wasn't certain if the sheen in her eyes was simply a reflection from the lamp or if his words had brought high emotion. "I would be proud to have your baby and incredibly happy to nurture him or her." She laid her hand alongside his cheek. "Come to me now, Nathan," she urged. "Please come to me. Don't hold back."

He kissed the lips she raised to his. She was everything he could ever hope for, and he no longer had reason to resist. She'd made her wishes extremely clear, and he wasn't going to disappoint her.

His touch found her slick and hot. He eased himself over her, and she accommodated his weight, welcoming him, helping him…she caught her breath and he hesitated. "I don't want to hurt you."

"Don't stop," she said against his shoulder. "Don't… stop. There's very little pain."

Burning with a painful need, he sank into her taut heated flesh, barely able to resist the ecstasy that swept through him and threatened to carry him away. But she pulled him close and wrapped herself around him in a way that made fire lick at his belly. All thoughts became incoherent. He lost himself in the sounds she made and the mesmerizing scents and sensations of their joining.

When she caught him around the neck and held her breath, he took his time, focused on maintaining and elongating her pleasure. Just as he thought he couldn't bear the delay another second, she gasped. Picking up the rhythm, he rocked against her until she cried out, and he followed her over the edge.

Nathan rolled beside her, trailing one hand across her abdomen to rest at her hip.

She lay on her back, her hair fanned across the pillow in a shiny golden skein, her breasts rising and falling as her breathing settled into a normal pattern.

Rolling her head to face him, she met his eyes. For a moment, his stomach felt as though he was perched on the edge of a precipice, ready to fall…. He couldn't bear it if she was embarrassed or humiliated or disgusted. His chest ached from not taking a breath. But then her lips parted and she smiled. A smile meant just for him. A lover's smile.

Something warm and wonderful blossomed near his heart. Something like hope.

"Tell me what you're thinking," she said.

He was thinking she was the most beautiful creature he'd ever laid eyes upon, but she didn't want to hear that. "I'm thinking I'm the most fortunate man on earth. The night we met you didn't know me from any of the others who asked for your hand in marriage. You had no idea what you were walking into, but you accepted my proposal. I don't know why. I can't fathom your reasoning. But I'm the man you chose."

She rolled to lay her palm against his cheek and look into his eyes. "You didn't know me, either."

"I know you're generous and kind. You don't really trust people, but you give of yourself anyway. Some of your actions puzzled me at first, but I see now that you've been working to make yourself belong and fit in."

Her frown created a little crease between her eyes. "I don't fit in."

"You're not like everyone else, and I don't want you to be. I like you just the way you are." He smoothed away the frown with his thumb. "You do belong. Right here with me. With our family."

She silenced him by covering his lips with her fingers.

He kissed the tips and then took them from his mouth. "There's a lot you don't want me to say. I can't say I like you the way you are. I can't tell you you're beautiful, even though you're so exquisite, I can barely breathe when I look at you."

"How would you like to be valued for your handsome face?"

"I wouldn't mind a compliment now and then."

That admission surprised Ella, and she studied him as though for the first time, running her index finger across the bridge of his straight nose and across his soft thick eyebrow. His children were handsome, and if she bore him a baby, it would be another fine-looking Lantry. The thought of having her own child filled her with longing and excitement. She'd never let her hopes and dreams extend that far before, and the thought of a future here with this man filled her with joy. Her feelings for him were confusing, but she wanted to hang on to the giddy pleasure.

"Well, you are a fine-looking man. I can't deny that. But it's the true character of who you are that speaks to me."

"And what is my character saying to you?"

"That you are ambitious. Steady and competent. You have a strict code of ethics and high expectations of those around you. You like to be in control, but you're not unfair. You're a loving father, concerned with the well-being of your children." She thought a moment before adding, "You always do the right thing, and that's important to you."

He seemed surprised by her words, but said nothing.

"Which would you rather hear?" she asked. "That you are a good man or that you are handsome?"

He grinned. "Only a vain man would say he preferred the compliments." He threaded his fingers through her tangled hair and pushed it away from her face. "I shall speak only of your character to woo you, then, because you are not vain."

He caught her knee and slid it over his hip to align their bodies. "You, Ella Lantry, are one of the smartest people I've ever met. You never judge anyone by their appearance or on a first impression. You are appreciative of the smallest thing, down to the most infinitesimal effort on another's part. You're quite curious. And you don't recognize your own value."

A niggle of panic rose up inside Ella at his intuitive assessment. She couldn't afford for him to look at her too astutely. She swallowed to keep fear from her voice. "Well-read on the subject of explorers and wines doesn't mean smart."

"I didn't say well educated, though you are. There's a difference. And I get the impression that you feel isolated, even here with our household or in a gathering."

She didn't care for his shrewd perceptions, but she understood that they made him a good leader. "I admire you," she admitted. "And everything about you. Your honesty and your ambition and even your idealism."

He raised his eyebrows. "Idealism?"

"Yes." And more than anything she wanted to be worthy of such an upright and principled man. He was as steady and unchanging as a rock in the middle of a raging river.

"No one has ever called me idealistic before."

"Perhaps I should stick to handsome."

He smiled, and this time it was a smile that crinkled his eyes and showed his teeth. He cupped her cheek and kissed her.

She ran her palm over his muscled shoulder and gently scraped her nails through the coarse hair on his chest. She liked everything about this man.

When the kiss ended, he said, "Lying here like this is new to me. Talking and enjoying each other, I mean. All along I was afraid to frighten you off. I didn't want to spoil what we had begun. Our marriage seemed so fragile."

It was more fragile than he imagined, but not for the reasons he thought. By taking this step and consummating their union, she hoped to strengthen their bond.

"Ella," he said, with an edge of seriousness that concerned her.

"You talk more than I might have anticipated," she said.

"I love you."

His words took her by surprise. *Love?* She blinked, hoping for comprehension, and sat up, taking the sheet with her to tuck around her breasts. She threaded her hair back from her face without looking at him. "You didn't have to say that."

"No one ever has to say it. I told you because I felt it, and it was right to say so."

He loved her? Once she'd believed her mother had loved her. But because the woman hadn't protected her from a life in the parlor house, she'd doubted her love— more now than even back then. After seeing children who were protected, she questioned what kind of love allowed a child to succumb to the fate Ella had. She'd seen the way Nathan safeguarded his children and planned for their futures. Her mother had never cared for her the same way.

Of course the love he declared had nothing to do with parents and children. It was love between a man and a woman.

No one had ever said those words to her before, and she didn't know how to receive them or to react.

He sat. "You don't have to say it," he told her. "I'm not expecting anything from you."

She recognized the pain in his voice, though. He wanted her to say it. "It's just…" she began and groped for words to explain. "I'm not sure I believe in that kind of love."

He was silent for a few minutes. The clock on the bureau ticked. "You don't have to say it," he assured her. "But just so you know…I will make you believe."

Chapter Sixteen

She remained facing away from him, not wanting him to see her eyes, concerned over what would be revealed in them.

If anyone could make her believe, it was him. If love actually existed, this man would know about it. But she feared her heart had already been hardened. She'd spent her childhood, and all the years since, perfecting her ability to not feel anything. Now her worst fear was of truly being the lifeless pretty doll she'd been created to be.

If anyone could help her change, Nathan Lantry could. After what she'd experienced and all he'd shared with her, she wanted to be a different person inside as well as out. Turning, she scooted closer and bracketed his face with her palm. "I believe in you."

She kissed him, and he snagged her around the waist and pulled her against him. She let the sheet fall away and straddled his lap, appreciating the surprise and delight on his face. "Let's not talk now," she suggested.

Within minutes, Nathan was speechless anyway.

Nathan couldn't remember a summer he'd enjoyed more. He had two cases that kept him working late several evenings a week, though when he arrived home, he didn't think of the job again until the following day. He rarely thought of Deborah, in fact, he placed their wedding photograph back in his bottom bureau drawer and never looked at it.

Ella couldn't have been more different from his first wife, from temperament and vitality to her cheerful conversations. Not only did she accept their physical relationship, she embraced it as a willing participant, even initiating lovemaking and speaking frankly. The first time she'd suggested they change position, he'd been so surprised, he couldn't remember what he'd answered. His reply must have been coherent, because the result had been a memorable experience.

He was behaving like a love-struck boy. Every time he looked at her fully clothed, he imagined the night before. As soon as he kissed her, he craved more. Simply her scent was enough to have him straining against his clothing.

"Perhaps I should behave with more decorum and… well, restraint," he said to her one evening after the children were asleep. She'd come to stand beside his desk in the study, and he'd urged her into his lap.

"Is that what you'd like from me?" she asked. "More modesty perhaps?"

"Not in a hundred years," he replied and slid his palm along her neck to draw her near for a kiss.

She offered him her mouth and greeted his seeking tongue with her own. "Are you content being *un*restrained?" she asked.

"Oh, yes," he replied against her lips.

"Perhaps we can agree that decorum has its place," she suggested. "And it's not in our bedroom."

He laughed. She was a vixen, this wife of his. Playful and seductive and so unexpectedly warm and willing. At times he couldn't believe his good fortune in finding her—and in her willingness to become his wife in all respects. Theirs was a relationship he'd never known.

The last Saturday in June, she was a bundle of nerves on the evening of their first dinner party. Even though she'd planned and cleaned and decorated and hired an additional cook and two maids for the event, she flushed pink and fluttered over the tables of food and the table settings.

"Ella, everything is perfect," he told her for the third time. "Stop worrying and calm down before you have the staff in a shambles."

She grasped his hands. "I know. I just don't want anything to spoil the evening or embarrass you."

"Try to keep your hands to yourself under the table this evening, then."

She laughed and her features relaxed. "I won't be sitting beside you, of course. I've arranged for you to be next to Mrs. Lawrence, and I'll be sitting beside Reverend Kane."

"Then definitely keep your hands above the table," he admonished.

"Nathan!" she gasped and pulled away.

He loved to make her laugh and joined her now.

She shook her head. "Don't you dare make eyes at me and make me think of this during dinner. If I unexplainably burst out laughing and make a fool of myself, I'll never forgive you."

"Yes, you will."

"I won't. I swear I won't."

"I guess you shouldn't look at me then."

The door chimes rang.

A shiver of panic ran up Ella's spine. She stared wide-eyed at Nathan.

"This evening is going to be fine. You've planned everything. Now let's go greet our guests." He caught her hand and led her toward the foyer.

The Olivers were the first to arrive, followed by the Evanses and the Iversons.

When the Bradburys arrived, Lena swept into the great room and eyed the crowd. Her gaze swooped from one person to the next with an expression that seemed contemptuous and almost angry. Ella made a point of crossing the room to greet her warmly. "I'm glad you could make it this evening."

"Why's that?" the other woman asked. "So you could rub my nose in the fact that you made a better match than I did?"

Taken aback, Ella worked to keep surprise from her voice and expression. She shot her glance to Tom, but he and Nathan were exchanging greetings and he hadn't overheard. "Not at all. I'm simply pleased you came."

Their husbands moved into the great room and Ella gestured for Lena to enter. Lena leaned sideways toward her, and Ella recognized the smell of liquor that clung to the woman. "You can drop the nicey-nice when it's just the two of us," she said, then spotted Nathan pouring the gentlemen drinks and made a beeline for the cabinet and glasses.

Exclaiming over the furnishings and decor in the great room, the other women hadn't noticed Ella's exchange with Lena. Ella joined them once again, but kept a wary eye on Lena.

Once Phoebe arrived, she discovered Ella's decorated folding screen and admired it.

"You've done your new husband proud," Betsy told her. "He must be pleased as punch that he found you."

Ella glanced across the room to where Nathan stood talking with Richard and Carl. He caught her look and gave her a nod of recognition. He was pleased to have married her, but she was pretty sure her decorating sense had nothing to do with his contentment. She smiled and he grinned and turned back to his conversation.

The maid appeared in the doorway and gestured to Ella. In the hallway, she discovered two more guests, Paul and Celeste Adams. "You came!" Ella exclaimed and rushed to Celeste's side.

"I'm sorry we're late," Celeste said. "I almost backed out, but Paul said we were coming or else."

Ella frowned. "You didn't want to come?"

"Oh, she wanted to come all right," Paul said. "She didn't think she had a fancy enough dress. I told her she's as pretty as any of the other women."

"And you were right, of course," Ella said. She hadn't stopped to think that Celeste's dresses may not be as elegant as those Ella owned. She'd always looked nice in Dodge City, though. It had been a requirement to dress appropriately for dinner. And she did look becoming in an off-the-shoulder emerald satin gown. "You look lovely."

"Do you think so?" Celeste smoothed her green skirts, self-consciously. As they moved into the other room and the lights touched Celeste's hair, Ella noticed that she'd stopped dying it black, and the roots were bright red. She'd arranged it so that the only place her true color showed was around her face, and she'd worn a piece of lace formed into a large flower in her tresses to draw attention away, but the outgrowth did look peculiar.

She took Celeste by the hand and led her toward a gathering. "You know Paul Adams and his wife, Celeste," she said by way of introductions.

The women seemed somewhat subdued by Celeste's arrival, but when Ella kept her arm linked with Celeste's and Nathan held a friendly conversation with Paul, they warmed to the newcomers. Ella hoped this was the introduction it would take for Celeste to be invited to join the choir and the women's gatherings. Celeste was a sweet, sincere woman, and she deserved to feel welcome.

Dinner came off without a hitch, and Ella's menu was well received. Her spirits were lifted, and her concerns banished until Lena carried a glass of amber liquid to the table. Tom gave her a hard look and moved the glass away from her. She waved him away, reached for the tumbler and drank the liquor. Betsy and Minnie cast her disapproving sidelong glances. Lena had entered into a more respected social station because of Tom, but she didn't seem to appreciate much about it.

Along with slices of rich chocolate-and-raspberry cake, coffee was served, and eventually the men moved to Nathan's study for cigars and brandy. The women clustered around the piano in anticipation of Ella's performance.

"What would you like to hear?" Ella asked.

"How about 'Camptown Races'?" Lena asked. She'd poured herself another drink and carried it with her. "Why do the men get to have all the fun? They're in there drinking and smoking, and we're supposed to be admiring Ella's gaudy folding screen." She pushed past Mildred Evans to take a seat on a divan. "It's a man's world, and there's no escaping it."

Ella grabbed a couple of pieces of sheet music and opened one. "We'll have a sing-along first. How's that?"

"That's just peachy," Lena said with a lazy sneer.

Celeste and Ella made eye contact, and Ella could tell the other girl was mortified by Lena's behavior. "Wait until you hear Celeste sing," Ella told the gathering. "She has a voice like an angel."

"I don't," Celeste denied, and her cheeks turned pink.

Ella played the opening measures of the song, and to her relief Celeste knew the words.

She sang, *"I'm thinking of Erin tonight, and the little white cot by the sea."* In her sweet contralto voice, Celeste caught the attention of the women and held it. *"Where Jennie, my darling, now dwells, the fairest and dearest to me."*

Betsy hurried to look over Ella's shoulder at the words and sang along, and on the second time through the others joined in.

"Play something we can dance to!" Lena called from the middle of the room. She now stood holding a drink in one hand and the framed photograph of the Lantry family in the other.

The men joined them then, and Tom had heard his wife's remark. "We'd better be going," he said to Nathan and took the frame from Lena, placing it back on the table. He nodded toward Ella. "Thank you for a lovely dinner."

"Ah, hell, let's stay and dance at least," Lena said. She took his hand and placed it on her hip. "Play something lively, Gabrielle!"

Ella's fingers froze on the keyboard. From the corner of her eye she caught Celeste's movement as she reached for Paul's hand and held it tightly. She lifted her gaze to the guests and noted the shocked and disgusted expressions on their faces.

Tom grabbed Lena forcefully around the waist and walked her out of the room. Nathan followed them into the hallway.

Ella wasn't sure what to do, but she didn't want to miss anything Lena might say as the couple departed, so she got up and dashed from the room. Behind her the women's voices droned in murmurs of surprise and disapproval.

"I apologize for my wife's behavior," Tom said to Nathan.

"Stop apologizing for me," Lena said from behind him.

Noticing Ella's approach, Tom gave her an embarrassed nod. "Thank you for your kind invitation, Mrs. Lantry. Dinner was excellent."

Ella felt terrible for the man. He'd been humiliated in front of his fellow business associates and their wives. She'd recognized that Lena had developed an attitude toward her and the other women, but obviously Ella hadn't taken her animosity seriously enough. She and Lena had never exactly been friends, but then theirs hadn't been that sort of relationship. The women who lived in the parlor house were discouraged from becoming friendly.

"If there's anything we can do for either of you, please let us know," Ella told him.

"Oh, *thank you,* Mrs. Lantry," Lena replied with oozing sarcasm. She escaped Tom's hold and leaned to grasp Nathan's tie. She held fast, urging him forward. "And thank *you*, Mr. Lantry. If I can be of any service to you…in any way at all," she emphasized. "You just let me know."

Nathan extricated his necktie from her grasp.

"Sorry, Nathan," Tom said before taking his wife firmly by the waist and hurrying her through the open doorway and toward the street.

Nathan closed the door. He looked at Ella, his consternation plain. "That was strange."

She nodded.

"She called you Gabrielle."

"Perhaps I remind her of someone."

"Was there a Gabrielle at Miss Haversham's?"

"I don't know where she got the name," she answered quickly.

"She's obviously a disturbed woman." He shook his head. "Poor Tom."

"Indeed."

Phoebe joined them then. "That was unfortunate," she said. "But don't worry, dear." She patted Ella's shoulder. "I started a conversation about the satire that Miss Alcott has been writing for the *Independent*. You can come back in and continue on at the piano as though nothing ever happened."

Ella glanced from Phoebe to Nathan. "I don't know. It seems wrong to pretend nothing happened."

"That's what one does in polite society," Phoebe assured her.

"But people will talk about it once they've left here.

Why not address it and move on?" She glanced at Nathan. "I'll defer to your judgment. What do you think is the right thing to do?"

He appeared thoughtful for a moment. "Facing an embarrassing situation is uncomfortable," he said with a nod to Phoebe.

She gave a self-satisfied nod in return.

"But," he added.

Phoebe's head swung back.

"I think that Ella might have the right idea in this case. Pretending won't make what happened go away, and the atmosphere will still be awkward."

Ella experienced relief and wasn't sure why. She didn't care who was right or wrong. She simply didn't want to make a mistake and cause more harm.

"I'll handle it," Nathan assured them and led the two women back into the great room.

Several of the guests turned their attention toward him expectantly.

"Mr. Bradbury apologized for his wife," he said. "He's an important part of our community, and right now he needs our friendship and support. Let's not desert him or look completely aside. I hope we can be available if the Bradburys need us."

Reverend Kane spoke his approval aloud, and most of the guests agreed their support would be readily available. Nathan encouraged Ella to go back to the piano, and the rest of the evening passed pleasantly.

Nathan didn't speak of the incident that evening when they changed and got into bed, but he was subdued. Ella draped her arm across his chest and snuggled close. He picked up her hand and kissed her fingers. "I'm so thankful to have you," he said softly.

Because of Lena's outburst, Ella's vulnerability and the deceit she lived with was utmost in her mind. Her husband wouldn't be thankful if he knew the truth. "I'm thankful to have you, too."

She rolled to face him. He took her in his arms, and the unpleasantness of the evening was forgotten.

Midmorning on Monday, the door chimes sounded, and Ella set down the tiny dress she'd been helping Grace put on her doll and went to answer the door.

Celeste stood on the shaded porch. "I hope I'm not bothering you."

"Of course not. Come in." Ella ushered her in out of the sun, took her parasol and hung it on the coat tree. "I'm delighted that you've come." She gestured toward the sitting room. "Please, come in and I'll make tea."

"Can I help you?"

"Yes, of course." Ella walked to the doorway. "I'll be right back, children. Mrs. Adams came calling, and I'm going to make a pot of tea."

Grace looked up, but as usual, said nothing. Robby continued to construct his blocks into a tower.

In the kitchen, Ella poured water from the pitcher that had been pumped earlier into the kettle and placed it on the stove. Charlotte had recently browned meat, and the scent remained in the air. The stove was still hot, and Ella added kindling.

Charlotte was nowhere in sight at the moment. Ella noticed the laundry tub and guessed she was out back.

"I told Paul the truth," Celeste said.

Not quite comprehending her meaning, Ella wiped her hands on a towel and turned to look at her. "About what?"

"About me. I told him the truth about Dodge City."

The information sank into Ella's mind and she blinked in shock. "You *what?*"

Chapter Seventeen

"I couldn't keep lying to Paul," Celeste said, her tone pleading with Ella to understand. "I couldn't take the chance that he'd find out some other way and be crushed. I couldn't hurt him like that. I didn't want my entire life to be a lie…so I told him."

Ella stared at the window without seeing the sunshine reflected on the panes. She stood like that until the kettle whistled and Celeste stepped around her to move it from the heat.

"What happened when you told him?" She hadn't noticed Celeste's bags on the front porch, but surely they were there right this moment. Celeste would likely be looking for work. For a place to stay. What had she been thinking?

"He cried some. Never saw a man cry before. It surely tore me up inside."

Ella tried to picture it, but couldn't.

"And then he thanked me for bein' truthful. He said it didn't make any difference to him what I did before, so long as I intended to be his wife now."

"It doesn't make a difference to him?" Ella sank onto a chair. Paul Adams knew. "He knows about all of us then."

"I didn't mean to spill the beans on everyone, but once he knew there was no Miss Haversham's, he figured out we'd all come from the same place."

Ella thought her heart would beat out of her chest. Visions of Nathan learning about her made her light-headed. She imagined the reactions of Betsy, Minnie and Phoebe, and a panicky feeling seized her. She thought of the past nights she'd spent in Nathan's arms and the relationship that had been developing between them. A trembling began in her limbs. She'd never been so afraid. "What if he tells people? What if he tells *Nathan?*"

"He won't. He said the others aren't his business. Only I'm his business, and he's settled my past in his head and we're going to put it behind us."

"Oh my," Ella said, now struggling to take a deep breath.

"I feel so much better," Celeste told her. "Like I've shrugged off a heavy load."

She felt better! A spark of anger ignited. "We were all in this together," Ella said and speared Celeste with a glare. "We came here to start a new life and not have to be who we were before. We committed to this secret together, all of us."

"I'm sorry if you feel as though I've let you down,"

Celeste said. "I just couldn't go on holding it in anymore. Pretending doesn't change us. Being truthful changes us. I'm not the same person anymore."

Ella didn't know what felt worse: being who she was or lying about who she was. She didn't enjoy lying any more than Celeste did. But the ruse had been the only way to carve out a new beginning.

She couldn't imagine Nathan accepting the news about her past and placidly saying it didn't make a difference. Nathan was proud and honorable and nothing had ever stained him or his reputation. She had his standing in the community to consider. His reputation had to remain unblemished for him to have a successful run for governor of the territory. His aspirations to hold a civil office would be ruined if the news got out that he'd married a courtesan.

She thought of his resolve to wait to initiate her to lovemaking because he believed she was as pure as his first wife had been. If he knew the truth, he'd be repulsed and disillusioned.

"I'm not the same person, either," Ella declared, but she wasn't certain. The only thing that had changed was her ability to feel. And at this point she didn't know now if feeling was such a great experience. She couldn't bear thinking of how much Nathan would suffer if he knew the truth about her.

She wanted to be the woman he believed she was.

Confused and frightened, she brought trembling hands up to cover her face.

"I didn't mean to hurt you," Celeste said softly. "I'm

not sorry I did it, but I didn't mean to make things harder for you."

Ella nodded and lowered her hands, determined to bring her emotions under control. "I know."

"Paul won't tell anyone."

"All right." Unconvinced, she got up and took a deep breath to gather her wits and courage. "Let's have tea."

Back in the sitting room, Grace had dragged two of her miniature chairs over to the tea table. Her undressed doll occupied one and she sat on the other. When Ella entered with the tea tray, Grace clapped her hands and smiled.

Ella offered Celeste a seat on the divan and tried to turn her thoughts away from Celeste's admission, but the unsettled sick feeling wasn't going away.

The other woman smoothed her skirts and sat comfortably on the divan.

Grace handed Ella the doll dress she'd abandoned, and Ella worked to pull the garment over the doll's head and fasten the miniature buttons.

"You're the first person who's come for tea," Ella told Celeste while handing the doll back to Grace, who promptly arranged her on her seat.

Celeste smiled and gestured to Grace and the doll. "Looks like these two ladies got here before me."

Grace appeared for all intents and purposes to have settled herself in for the duration of their tea, and Ella didn't see any reason she shouldn't join them.

"I'd better get more cups." Ella hurried out, returning with the cups and a second small pitcher of cream.

She poured tea into four cups, making Grace's and the dolls' only half-full. She had brought a cup of milk for Robby.

Grace looked at the plate of cookies expectantly, her gaze turning up to Ella.

"What would you like, Grace?"

The child pointed to the plate.

"What are those?"

Grace simply stared at the treats.

"Robby, would you like a cookie and milk?"

Robby dropped a block and got to his feet. "Cookie, please!"

She waited until he'd taken a seat on the floor before handing him a cookie and sitting the cup beside him. He bit into the treat immediately.

"Grace, would you like a cookie?" Ella asked.

The little girl nodded.

After a moment of frustrating silence, Ella handed her a cookie and indicated the cup of milky sweetened tea. "There you go then."

Celeste glanced from Grace to Ella. "Did you bake these?"

"No, Charlotte did. She does most of the cooking, and she's an excellent baker."

"Maybe she would share the recipe."

"I'm sure she wouldn't min—"

"Wanna cookie, Dolly? You can have part of mine. There, don't cwy."

In surprise, Ella glanced at Grace, who had spoken to the doll seated beside her.

"I help-ded Miss Charlotte make these, and it was hawd work," she said. "Do you love the sugah on top? I sprinkled it my own self."

Having never heard Grace's childish little voice before, Ella listened, enthralled. Her heart rate increased with excitement. Celeste was looking at Ella curiously.

Ella leaned over to whisper in her ear. "She never speaks. Not to us, anyway. Nathan told me he'd heard her talking to her dolls while she was playing in her room, but this is the first I've heard her voice."

Celeste smiled, but both women were careful not to stare at Grace and make her self-conscious.

"Charlotte has quite a few excellent recipes she can share," Ella said to Celeste. "She's been showing me how to do a little cooking, so I can help out more when she's not here."

Grace picked up the piece of cookie she'd set in front of the doll and nibbled it gone.

"Is your cookie all gone, Dolly?" Ella asked, speaking directly to the doll. "Perhaps you'd like another?"

Grace glanced from her doll to Ella and back, her eyebrows raised as though surprised that an adult was talking to her doll.

Ella broke a cookie in half and placed it in front of the doll. "There are plenty, so enjoy another one, won't you? How about you, Celeste?"

"I'd love another one, thanks."

Ella didn't really know if what she was doing was beneficial, but Grace's conversation with the doll felt like their first real communication, so she didn't mind if the chat was out of the ordinary.

"Don't buwn your tongue on your tea," Grace cautioned the doll and took a sip of hers.

As delighted as Ella was to hear Grace talk, her pleasure was overshadowed by a dark cloud now that Celeste had told Paul the truth about their background. It was entirely possible that her days here were numbered, and the thought was crushing.

They finished their tea and Charlotte arrived to take the trays. Ella introduced her to Celeste and asked the cook if she would be kind enough to share recipes. Charlotte was happy to oblige and promised a handful the following week.

Before long, Ella saw the other woman to the door and wished her a good day.

"It's going to be all right," Celeste assured her. "Paul will keep our secret, I'm convinced."

Ella nodded. "I hope so."

"He will. Don't you worry about it, okay? I'll see you on Thursday."

"Thursday?"

"It's Independence Day. The town was already abuzz this morning."

"Oh, yes, of course." She'd heard talk of the celebration for weeks now, and Nathan had been working on the speech he would give for the city council and the crowd on that morning. Ella had never attended anything of the sort. She should be looking forward to the festivities, but worry was already set into motion and her dark cloud of concern wasn't going anywhere.

Ella did her best to stay busy and keep her mind occupied. That evening, she shared with Nathan how Grace had spoken to the doll. After planning what she and the children would wear on Independence Day, she arranged tea parties in the nursery on Tuesday and Wednesday afternoons. Both days, Grace carried on a conversation with her doll, still never replying to anything Ella said.

Robby was always congenial and willing to participate in any games or readings Ella presented. Instructing him on the piano was a challenge, because he simply wanted to bang the keys in any fashion that suited him, but she kept working until he could point out middle C.

The more attached to and involved with the children she grew, the more worrisome thoughts of her history being discovered became. At night she lay awake beside Nathan, his breathing even and peaceful, while her imagination conjured up scenarios in which Paul Adams paid her husband a visit and told him all he knew.

How was it that Paul had accepted the truth without turning Celeste away? Being around the women of Sweetwater had taught her the strict codes of conduct and propriety suitable for good people. Anything less— anything as lewd as Ella's previous life would be unacceptable. A woman's gentility reflected on her husband, and only the highest order of modesty and virtuousness was tolerated.

If the truth came to light, Nathan's good name would be ruined. In the wee hours of the morning, just as the first rays of dawn reached their bedroom windows and as the early and exuberant celebrants fired guns and set off fireworks in the distance, Ella wondered if perhaps she should tell Nathan before he learned about Dodge City or the parlor house from Paul.

The gunfire woke him, and he rolled his head toward her, opening his eyes and gazing into hers. "Good morning."

His voice was low and gravelly from sleep.

"Good morning," she replied.

"How is it you're as lovely first thing in the morning as you were the night before? Sometimes I think I must have dreamed you, because no man is this fortunate."

She gave him a smile. "I'm not moved by flattery, as you well know."

"Ah, fortunate for me, I've learned how to move you." He scooted closer to kiss her bare shoulder and her collarbone, his lips creating tingling shivers of delight.

He took her in his arms, bringing their bodies in alignment beneath the sheet.

"Papa!" The shout was followed by a loud rap on the closed door.

Nathan gave her a look of regret. "This will have to wait until tonight," he promised, then called over his shoulder, "What is it, Christopher?"

The door flew open. "Did you hear the firecrackers? They've begun celebrating!"

Nathan gave Ella a quick kiss and sat up. "People fire their weapons and set off fireworks all day long on

Independence Day. Remember? Those sounds you heard are neighbors starting the day early."

"I can't wait for the fireworks," the boy said.

"Neither can I," Nathan replied. "That's my favorite part." He glanced at Ella. "How about you? What's your favorite part of Independence Day?"

"I don't know yet. This will be my first."

A line formed between the boy's brows. "But the Fourth of July comes every year."

She had to be more careful about how she said things, because she hated adding more lies to her relationships. "Well, I was always in school."

"Even on the weekend?" he asked in disbelief.

"She lived at an academy," Nathan explained.

"You'll like Independence Day," Christopher assured her, his face solemn. "The speeches and stuff are kinda boring. But after that everything is fun."

Nathan raised his eyebrows and looked from Ella to his son, who continued talking, unaware that he'd insulted his father. "Last year there was a war dance," Christopher went on. "What tribe were they, Papa?"

"Cree, I believe," Nathan replied.

"They wore long feathers." Christopher gestured with drawn-out motions from both sides of his head. "And beaded moccasins and fur leggings."

"There were Cheyenne dancers, too," Nathan added.

"They even have feathers on their tomahawks," the boy told her. "And there are lots of games for anybody who wants t'play, like croquet—but mostly the girls do that—and baseball and wheelbarrow races. And there are prizes, too. Right, Papa?"

"That's right. Dress in old clothes if you want to climb the greased pole," Nathan told Ella with a grin. "There'll be a five-dollar bill right on top."

She gave him a skeptical glance, and he winked.

"Can I try to climb the pole this time, Papa?" Christopher asked.

"Sure you can." He glanced at Ella again. "I have to wear a suit for the opening oration and the reading of the Declaration of Independence, but I'll come back and change afterward. We don't want to worry about our clothing. The games get messy. Then we'll come home and clean up before the fireworks this evening. Let us get up and dressed now."

The boy grinned and shot out of the room.

Already the day was promising to be one of the warmest of the summer. Ella had chosen a pale pink cotton dress for herself. Streamers of matching ribbons fluttered from her wide-brimmed straw hat.

She had selected a lightweight green-striped dress for Grace, and helped Robby don a white shirt and knee-length pants. She'd purchased a straw hat for him. He frowned and pouted when she placed it on his head.

"It will keep the sun from your eyes," she assured him. "And you look quite dashing in it." She picked him up and showed him his reflection in the hall mirror.

He appeared dubious, but soon forgot his uncertainty when his father called from below, "Who wants to ride in the buggy for the parade?"

Robby squirmed from her arms and took the stairs as quickly as his short little legs would allow. "Me am, Papa!"

Wearing her frilly bonnet, Grace joined Ella and reached for her hand before they descended the stairs. The gesture of trust and acceptance touched Ella.

"Whatever is wrong?" Nathan asked from where he stood in the foyer with Robby on one arm, his own hat in his other hand. Concern etched his handsome brow.

Ella shook her head, concerned that she'd shown emotion plain enough for her husband to notice. "Nothing is wrong. I'm just happy."

"Well, you both look as sweet as ice cream," he assured them. "You'll be the prettiest girls there."

Grace smiled up at her, and Ella returned her look of happiness. She was going to enjoy this day, regardless of the worry that niggled at her conscience. The celebration was important to the children and to Nathan, and they were important to her.

This was Independence Day, after all, and freedom was something she was determined to appreciate.

Chapter Eighteen

Christopher wore a pair of dungarees and a short-sleeved shirt and looked for all the world as though he was setting off on an adventure. And indeed he was, Ella realized shortly after leaving the house.

The neighborhood bustled with activity as families set out for Main Street.

All manner of gaily decorated conveyances waited on the outermost road. Nathan led them to an open wagon that was in line before the fire department's water wagon. It was another twenty-five minutes before all the officials had boarded the buggies and wagons. Once all were in place, the parade began, with the band proudly leading the way.

Men, women and children lined the thoroughfare, cheering and waving. "I never realized there were so many people in Sweetwater," Ella said.

"A lot of them live on surrounding ranches and farms,

plus people come from all the nearby towns for the celebration."

Once they reached the main thoroughfare, the transformation was breathtaking. Every building along Main Street had been draped in red, white and blue bunting swags that hung from the edges of roofs and railings. American flags flapped in the sunlight.

The musicians were first to break formation and carry their instruments toward another destination.

An enormous grandstand had been constructed at the east end of town, and its covered roof sported patriotic flags. At the forefront stood a podium, draped with more bright bunting. Citizens were already jostling for places to stand at the front of the crowd.

Nathan checked his watch. "Fifteen more minutes. You'll stand on the platform with me, Ella." He scanned the boardwalk and storefronts, then waved. "There's Mrs. Shippen. The children will join her until the speeches are over."

"I could stay here with them," she offered.

"Your place is beside me," he replied with a proud tilt of his head.

Mrs. Shippen looked cheerful wearing a white dress with red piping and a feathered hat. She gathered the children and guided them toward a boardwalk.

Several Indians dressed as Christopher had described stood on the platform and greeted Nathan as he and Ella climbed the newly constructed wooden stairs.

The black-haired men observed Ella with solemn obsidian gazes. Having never seen an Indian up close, these were particularly intimidating in their quilled and beaded shirts and their feathered headdresses. Obviously they were friendly or they wouldn't be part of the celebration, but she stood close to Nathan all the same. A canvas awning protected them from the sun, with only the foremost point of the podium exposed.

A tall silver-haired man joined them, and Ella was introduced to the mayor and his wife.

The band members, all attired in red jackets and white shirts with blue bow ties, gathered at the side of the platform, placing themselves in order.

Mayor Simpson signaled the band leader, and the first patriotic piece of music burst from the instruments and immediately caught the crowd's attention. While the musicians played exuberantly, people gathered from all the side avenues and trailed from the stores, filling the street.

The mayor stepped up to welcome everyone and declare the festivities open. He introduced Nathan next, and Nathan took his place, opening a pamphlet he took from inside his jacket.

"One hundred and nine years ago this morning, George the Third was King of Great Britain and Ireland and of the British Colonies in North America. Before the sun set that day the fairest portion of his North American colonists had forsworn their allegiance and declared their independence."

A cheer rose from the crowd, and Nathan paused until they quieted. "It's only fitting and proper that on the anniversary of such a memorable day that we should indulge in retrospection and celebrate our liberties."

Again the people clapped and cried out with excitement.

Ella glanced at the sheaf of handwritten pages on the podium, wondering how long it would take her husband to get through his oration if he was interrupted after each sentence.

Her gaze wandered to Mrs. Shippen and the children to find Christopher attentively watching the Indians, and Robby and another small child looking at something the other boy held.

She had plenty of time to scan the people in the audience and find nearly everyone she knew. Celeste caught her eye and gave her a barely perceptible wave. Ella smiled. She focused on Paul, standing tall in the morning sun without a hat. He wore a pair of faded overalls, apparently ready for the day of games.

He glanced down at Celeste, and Ella noticed that their hands were clasped. He drew hers upward and touched his lips to her fingers in an intimate sign of affection. His wife gave him an adoring smile.

Ella's heart tripped at the sight. Nathan had declared his love for her. She'd heard him, but she'd put those words from her mind and hadn't wanted to think about it. Why was that?

Didn't she believe him? She had no reason not to.

Did she doubt her worthiness? Yes.

Nathan believed he loved her, but he didn't really

know her. He'd fallen in love with the image she'd projected, not the real Ella.

She took her attention back to Celeste and Paul in the crowd. At the time Ella had been perturbed with her for betraying their confidence, but Celeste hadn't carried the lie into her marriage and based their relationship on a mirage.

Paul loved her, regardless of her past. He would keep the secret, no worries there. She noticed Mildred Evans standing with her son, Jimmy, and noted Phoebe and Richard Crandall in the gathering.

Nathan's voice carried as he said, "Today we rejoice and congratulate each other that we have lived to see the auspicious opening of another Independence Day, a day of events that commemorates that this generation of Americans have not forgotten the teachings of our fathers."

Nathan adhered to a strict code of ethics, and that's what made him the man he was. His sense of duty and of idealism and good judgment were the reasons he stood here today, respected by his peers and all the people of the territory. He would make an excellent governor.

The sense of shame that plagued her draped a pallor over the sunny morning and deflated her mood. She would not be standing on this platform if Nathan knew who she really was.

She would not be standing here if the people of the Wyoming Territory—especially the citizens of Sweetwater—knew the truth about who she was. His acceptance of her had risked all he'd worked for—all he stood for. And she'd led him to the hazard without his knowledge.

She had wanted freedom and a normal life so badly that any means had been acceptable at the time.

The crowd applauded in earnest, cheers and whistles interrupting her thoughts. Nathan had finished his speech. He waved with a broad smile and introduced Mayor Simpson, who would be reading the Declaration of Independence.

The major took the podium and began the reading. Nathan joined her, slipping his hand into hers.

"You were brilliant," she whispered.

He grinned.

Once the mayor had finished, Reverend Kane addressed the crowd and said a prayer of thanks for their freedom and petitioned God to safely see them through the events of the day.

"I'm heading home to change," Nathan told her.

"Wait," she told him. "There's one more thing you have to stick around for."

"What is it?"

"You'll see. Stay right here." She left him at the corner of the grandstand and held her hem while she climbed the stairs.

The other women were gathering, and Mildred supervised getting them into two straight rows. From her place on the riser in the back row, Ella searched the waiting crowd and found Nathan.

Mildred gave a signal, and the pianist behind them played the opening measures. The ladies came in right on time. *"O-oh, say can you see by the dawn's early light."*

The crowd hushed in reverence for the song and the women's voices raised in three-part harmony. Ella had never participated in anything so monumental or important, and for those moments while she sang her alto harmony, she felt part of something grand. Something wholesome and worthy.

"Blest with victory and peace, may the heav'n rescued land praise the Power that hath made and preserved us a nation."

With a catch in her chest and tears in her eyes, she sang the last lines. Their voices trailed away and a full minute of silence elapsed. The moment seemed suspended in sunshine.

Finally, a few at a time, the people in the crowd applauded. The women hugged and congratulated one another on a job well done, and Ella made her way down the stairs to where Nathan waited.

He opened his arms and hugged her. "I'm so proud of you."

Within his embrace the world felt right. Nothing but the larger picture mattered in that moment. Their freedom, their health and their love for each other were all that counted for anything. "Thanks for the surprise," he said.

She eased away and gave him a smile.

"I'll meet you in front of the bank in twenty minutes," he said then.

"I'll be there."

She located Mrs. Shippen and gathered the children, then guided them through the dispersing crowd to the other side of the street, where a Cheyenne woman sold trinkets. She bought something for each of the children.

"Did you hear?" Betsy asked, coming up beside her.

"Hear what?"

"Tom Bradbury has had enough of his new wife's boorish behavior. She's been staying at the hotel for the past few nights." She leaned in closer and whispered, "The desk clerk told James Evans that she entertained a guest in her room last night." She leaned back and glanced around, then finished, "A *male* guest."

Ella absorbed the information with a dread that refueled her anxiety. Lena's behavior was likely to start a problem for all the women from Dodge City. "I'm sorry to hear that."

"Scandalous is what it is."

Ella nodded. Yes, the good people of this town were likely scandalized by Lena's behavior.

"She's made a fool of poor Tom, who was only looking for a woman of good character and quality."

Ella's stomach quivered. "He's a good man."

"I haven't seen him yet this morning," Betsy added. "He's probably ashamed to show his face."

"He has nothing to be ashamed of," Ella pointed out.

"Except being drawn into a shocking situation," Betsy replied.

Ella spotted Nathan making his way toward her, being greeted by and shaking hands with townspeople. "Here's Nathan. Excuse me."

She'd never seen him dressed in dungarees and a soft cotton shirt before, and she liked his casual appearance.

"Papa!" Christopher called, tugging on his father's hand. "The mule race is going to start! We hafta go *now!*"

"We can't be late for that," Nathan agreed. He swooped Robby up onto his shoulders and led the family toward the playing fields and tracks.

The mule trotting race was one of the funniest things Ella had ever seen. After a few feet, one of the mules refused to budge, and no amount of yelling or urging by the youth on its back made a difference. Another animal took a deviant route along the path where the bystanders lined the track. Three others actually trotted, though one mule's impossibly large rider slowed the animal down considerably.

The winner won a five-dollar purse and his mule was draped with a wreath made of grapevine entwined with clover.

To Christopher's delight, Nathan entered the one-fourth-mile footrace. Ella and the children stood near the finish line and cheered as he finished third. He accepted his five-dollar prize with a broad grin.

Afterward they bought sandwiches and drinks from a stand and ate in the shade of a grove of trees Nathan said were honey locusts. The fragrant grass was cool and soft beneath them. Christopher pulled a handbill from his pocket and unfolded it. "What time is it? The U.S. Regulars drill is at one o'clock."

"We have a few minutes." Nathan glanced at Ella. "It seems we're not going to miss anything."

"I wouldn't want to miss a moment," she answered with a smile. She'd never experienced an adventure like this. The spirit of goodwill that permeated the community along with the excitement of children and adults alike was contagious.

Firearms reverberated and popping explosions went off regularly. On the grass nearby lay the remains of spent firecrackers.

"Every dog in Sweetwater is hiding under a porch," Nathan said. Ella had noticed that a few of the nearby horses had been startled by the noise, as well.

"Let's go," Christopher urged.

The Regulars marched and fired their rifles into the air with another earsplitting volley. Afterward, the Cheyenne dancers performed, and they were every bit as colorful and entertaining as Christopher had described.

Christopher attempted to climb the greased pole, but came away from the effort disappointed. Nathan gave him his five-dollar winnings for making a good attempt, and the lad's face brightened. Nathan asked Grace to be his partner in a sack race, and they lagged far behind the others, but the little girl laughed each time she fell and thoroughly enjoyed herself.

"Want to try?" Nathan asked Ella.

"Oh, goodness, no." She'd seen the others spilling onto

the grass with a complete lack of dignity and couldn't see herself doing the same.

"I'll snatch a bag so we can practice first," he told her. "The trick is for me to take smaller strides so you can keep up. Look, Celeste is racing."

Indeed, Celeste had one leg in a gunny sack as she ran alongside her much-taller husband. Her bonnet fell back, revealing that her red hair had grown out even farther, the black ends she'd tied back, flying loose.

Seeing her reminded Ella of the tentative ribbons that bound her into marriage with Nathan. She came to the conclusion at that moment that she had to tell him everything. She couldn't live her life waiting for those bonds to come undone and the sky to come crashing down on her. And, she realized, like Celeste, she could no longer lie to the man she loved.

As he stood waiting for her reply, she looked up at him. His eyes twinkled with amusement and the light of challenge. Nathan turned everything she knew about the human race—and about men especially—upside down and sideways. He was truthful, honorable, steady and fair, and she loved him with all of her being.

She'd never allowed herself to feel before coming to this place and meeting this man and getting to know his community. She'd felt a slim attachment to a few people, including her mother and her tutor, but because they weren't committed to her, she had to keep feelings locked away. She'd learned the hard way that emotion made a person vulnerable. She had no experience with that kind of exposure.

Nathan had been brave enough to make himself vulnerable. Perhaps it was time she stopped holding herself apart and let herself feel.

"All right." She took off her hat, enjoying the look of surprise and pleasure that came over his features.

After asking Rowena Templeton to look out for the children, he did as promised and snagged a gunnysack, leading her away from the festivities. He coached her slowly until they could run without tripping each other, and then they made their way to the course for the next race and waited their turn.

Finally, they took their places at the starting line.

"Nathan," she said softly.

He glanced down at her expectantly. "Don't be nervous."

"I love you."

Chapter Nineteen

Nathan's world tilted crazily, and in the midst of all the commotion, his focus narrowed down to Ella's dear face and the words she'd uttered.

She looked at him with such tender openness, he wanted to kiss her and take her in his arms right there. Her timing stank. The most exquisite woman he'd ever laid eyes on, who was also kind and generous and appreciative of every last thing, this woman who'd taken his heart, loved him in return. Her love was the dearest gift he'd ever been given.

"Five!" the starter called. "Four."

He remembered the promise he'd made her that morning. "Tonight, Mrs. Lantry."

She smiled.

"Two! One!" The pistol fired into the air, and they turned their attention to their feet and legs, keeping their stride and balance even.

Nathan held her firmly against his side. If she did lose her footing, he could carry her until she regained her balance. He was delighted to note that as couples stumbled and fell, they took the lead and finished ahead of the remaining competitors.

Gasping for air, Ella laughed and hugged him around the waist. "What did we win?"

The judge declared them the winners and pointed toward a rows of tables. "Pick your prize."

The prizes were golden-crusted pies and delicately frosted cakes. Ella's eyes lit up.

"What's your favorite?" Nathan asked.

"I'm not sure." She studied the arrangement as though she was selecting a diamond ring. "I've never tasted peach pie. It looks awfully good."

"They're warm from the sun," he told her, picking it up and carrying it on his open palm. "Let's go share our prize."

They gathered the children and ate the delectably sweet slices without plates or forks, which the children found hilarious. Ella even had a second piece.

"So what do you think of peach pie?" Nathan asked.

Her face was flushed, and he located her hat and plopped it on her head. She gave him a sweet smile. "I can only think of one thing better."

"I love you, Ella."

"And I love you, Nathan."

The words spoken in her deep sultry voice rocked him. Images of the coming night flashed into his head, and his insides melted. There would be fireworks and dancing first, but after that... He couldn't wait to get her home. How had he been so fortunate as to acquire a wife like Ella?

By sundown, the children were exhausted, but fidgety and talkative in anticipation of the fireworks. After a day of activity in the sun, they trudged home to bathe and dress in fresh clothing. Robby fell asleep after his quick bath, and Nathan dressed him while he slept. Ella buttoned Grace into a blue dress with a white pinafore.

Christopher dressed himself and Nathan combed his hair. Robby slept on his father's shoulder as they walked toward the field where the fireworks would be displayed. Christopher and Ella carried soft old blankets that they spread out once they got there. Robby revived as soon as Nathan laid him down. He looked around and sat up with an expectant expression. One side of his hair stood up where it had dried while he slept with his head against Nathan's collar. Ella leaned over and attempted to smooth it down.

Nathan asked Grace and Christopher to lie down for a little quiet time before the fireworks display, and they obediently rested on the blankets.

He took Ella's hand. "I can't recall a day I've enjoyed as much as this one, and it's because you're here."

She loved the feel of his strong hard fingers. The look of devotion in his eyes spoke to her soul and flooded her with regret. She prayed he would feel the same way about her once she'd told him about her past, but she had to be prepared for the worst. "I've never spent a day like this," she told him. "I've never before had a family." She glanced at the children. "Thank you for letting me be part of today."

"You're my wife now," he told her. "You're an important part of everything." He hugged her against his side and kissed the top of her head. His deep voice resonated through his chest when he said gruffly, "I'm the one who should be thanking you."

She rested her hand against the front of his shirt.

"Maybe by this time next year, we'll have another little Lantry joining us," he whispered against her ear.

The thought terrified and thrilled her at the same time.

They rested like that while the stars popped out in the heavens and townspeople gathered on their separate squares until the hillside looked like a patchwork quilt under the bright moon.

Ella had watched sporadic fireworks from the balcony at the parlor house on July Fourth evenings, but the only reason she knew the night was a holiday was because the house was so quiet. A few regulars came in during the late hours, but Ansel Murdock had never visited her. He'd been with his family, attending a celebration similar to this one, she suspected.

That whole part of her life seemed so distant now, she could hardly relate it with her time in Sweetwater. If only Gabrielle had never existed and that time had never happened. If only she'd had an upbringing like the people here…like these children. Safe and protected from unpleasantness and crudity. At the time she'd been growing up and living in the parlor house, she hadn't known anything different. That life had seemed normal. It hadn't been until later, when she heard the other girls talk of families and plans to leave and start new, until she'd become aware that other young women could shop and walk through town without scorn that the reality of her sordid existence came into focus.

Colorful bursts lit the night sky to the appreciative exclamations of all, including Ella, who watched with wonder and fascination. She turned to observe Nathan's strong handsome profile tilted upward. She was going to do the right thing and tell him the truth.

If he truly loved her the way she hoped he loved her, her past would make no difference. They would spend their years together, raising children and attending Independence Day celebrations until they were old.

Eventually, the last explosion lit the sky, the embers fading as they fell toward earth. She tucked away the memory of this day like a precious keepsake.

Tents had been erected around a square consisting of several wooden platforms assembled for dancing and the bands. "The tents are for sleeping children," Nathan told her. "The women take turns sitting with them."

"I'll take a turn," she offered quickly.

He directed her to Sarah Pickering, who sat at the opening to a tent. Ella's assignment was the first time slot, so she and Nathan settled Grace and Robby down on their blankets and she took her turn. She had a baby in her charge, and he fussed until she awkwardly picked him up and rocked him in her arms.

The little fellow was surprisingly heavy, but soft and warm and smelled like milk and talcum powder. She'd never held a baby before and hoped she didn't do something wrong, but his eyelids closed and he drifted into peaceful sleep. The feel of his plump little body lying against her breast brought untested mothering instincts to life. He had tiny features, a wet rosebud mouth and a soft tuft of hair atop his head. He was the sweetest thing she'd ever held. Thoughts of holding a baby of her own were only natural.

Maybe by this time next year, we'll have another little Lantry joining us, Nathan had said. It was her dearest wish, next to remaining with the Lantrys in Sweetwater.

On the hour, a young woman who introduced herself as Donetta Jones and the baby's mother arrived to relieve her. Ella grudgingly handed her the baby and went back out into the night to find Nathan and Christopher. They were seated on planks that ran alongside the dance floors.

"Here she is," Nathan said with a smile.

"I held a baby," she said softly.

Nathan gave her a smile. "How was it?"

"Nice," she replied.

"May I have this dance?" Christopher asked as though he'd been coached.

She took his hand and they found an opening among the couples moving to the music. Eventually, Nathan took

Christopher to the tent to join his sister and brother for sleep and returned to Ella.

He took her elbow and led her to the dance floor, where they fell into step. Ella hummed along with "Sweet Genevieve."

"We could take your phonograph down by the stream and dance under the stars later tonight," Nathan said.

She leaned back and stared up at him. "What a romantic idea!"

"I have a lot of romantic ideas in my head right now," he told her.

Heart swelling, she rested her head against his shoulder. After another song, the tempo changed, and a rousing rendition of "Little Brown Jug" ensued. "I wonder what the ladies are thinking of this song," Ella said to Nathan with a laugh. "I'm sure it's highly improper."

She followed Nathan's gaze to the sidelines where Tom Bradbury sat on the planks with a few other men. This was the first time she'd seen him all day, and his presence at the evening festivities surprised her.

Nathan drew a handkerchief from his pocket and dabbed his forehead. "There's beer in a tent behind the bandstand," he said. "I think I'll head back there for a mug. Do you want anything?"

"You go ahead. I'll join the ladies for lemonade."

Nathan walked around the deserted bandstand, away from the noise of the dancers and the music.

"I've been wondering where you were."

He turned at the voice and squinted into the darkness.

Lena Bradbury strolled toward him. He hadn't seen her all day or evening, so her appearance now surprised him. "If you're looking for Tom, he's back there by the dancers."

"I was looking for you."

"What for?"

She walked right in front of him, blocking his path and stood uncomfortably close. "A *diversion,* I guess you could say."

Nathan took a step back, but she took a step forward. He glanced around. Anyone could be coming this way and see them.

She reached out and laid her hand on the front of his shirt in a flirtatious gesture. "Nervous about something?"

He took her wrist and removed her hand. "This is inappropriate, Mrs. Bradbury."

"No one has to know," she said. "What do you say we slip a little farther away from the crowd and…get to know each other better?"

"You're my friend's wife, and even if you weren't, I'm a married man." He detached himself from her hold again and moved away.

"Well, aren't you the pious one?" She twirled a tress of hair around her index finger and glared at him in the light from the moon and the lanterns strung along the path. "Think you're too good for me, do you?"

"Of course not. But Tom's a good man. He can make you happy if you give him a chance."

She laughed derisively. "There are too damned many

good men in this town if you ask me. The bad boys are a whole lot more fun."

"Why did you marry him if you weren't going to try to make your marriage work?" he asked. "Why'd you come here at all if you didn't want to settle down and be a wife?" He changed his mind about the beer and turned back toward the festivities. "Excuse me. My wife is waiting."

"Oh my, yes, you're such a gentleman," she said. "Hurry back to your delicate flower before she wilts." And then she called a little louder as he walked away, "Or until she turns her attentions on some *richer* man." She followed him. "She likes the rich ones, she does. Oh, yes. Only the best for Gabrielle."

Nathan had reached the clearing where the dance floor and the band was, and the musicians paused between songs, so Lena's next words rang out from behind him.

"All of you think you're so much better than I am. You and your fancy houses and your carriages and your clothes and your ridiculous parties."

In front of him, people turned to see who was shouting.

He paused at the corner of the dance floor.

Murmurs carried through the crowd.

Nathan turned his head and found Tom, who was now slowly rising from the bench. The man had already been forced to suffer enough indignities. What was wrong with that woman?

"Lena," a woman said in a kind tone. "Why don't you come with me, and we'll go somewhere and talk?"

He recognized Rita Thomas, one of the other women who'd come West with the group of brides. She'd married the liveryman.

"What are we going to talk about?" Lena asked. "Old times?"

Rita paused in front of her.

Nathan searched for Ella, finding his wife standing not far from where he'd left her, her hands clasped in front of her, wearing a look of distress.

"Maybe if you gave your friends a chance," Nathan said. "You'd see that they want to help you."

"Friends?" she asked, her voice shrill. "Those— *women*—are not my friends. They were the competition where we came from, and they're the competition here. Nothing changed—except the men in our beds."

Someone gasped.

Rita reached for Lena, attempting to comfort or silence her, he wasn't sure which, and Lena jerked away from her touch. "Get your hands off me! You're no better than *her*." Lena jerked her head in the direction where Ella stood. "You all think you're better than me. All of you. Well, you're *not!*"

She stood in a circle of light from a nearby lantern, her posture stiff with anger. She turned her rage on Nathan. "*You,* Mr. High and Mighty city attorney. You're just like every other man who ever set eyes on that woman. You're blinded by her French perfume and that sensuous voice she has perfected." Lena closed the distance that separated her from Nathan and glared up at him. "You're drawn to that silken pale hair and her soft delicate skin. Do you have any idea how much it costs to make a woman look like that? Nothing was ever spared on her, because she was special."

"That's enough, Lena." Celeste Adams had left her husband's side and come to urge Lena away from Nathan and into silence. "Come with me."

"*This* one," Lena said, shaking her finger at Celeste, "never escaped a Friday night without a black eye, so she's pleased as punch to be here, hobnobbing with the likes of you."

"Lena, *shut up*," Celeste said in earnest, her glare a warning.

"But not our lovely Gabrielle. Oh no, not our rose among the thorns. Not our musically gifted *lady,* the one reserved for only the richest client. No, not our beautiful French *whore*."

The word left stunned silence in its wake.

Lena laughed then. An odious sound that made the bystanders visibly uncomfortable. "You're all so easily duped." She raked a glance from one shocked face to the next. "You brought a wagonload of whores into your uppity little town! All the way from Dodge City, Kansas, yes-sir-ee, where the cowpokes never stop piling in on Saturday night and the wind never stops blowing up dust, brought them directly to your doorstep. And you married us!" she added gleefully, then laughed again.

She rounded on Nathan and looked him in the eye. "You, Mr. Big Shot Councilman, married yourself a whore."

Her words sank into Nathan's mind, swimming

about in confusion, seeking verification…while Rita and Celeste glared at Lena…and a buzz moved through the crowd. He sought Ella and found she'd moved closer, but still stood a dozen yards away, frozen to the spot, staring at him with a look of dread that drove shards of unease into his heart.

A hundred little pieces of a bigger puzzle swirled into place and snagged his awareness. Ella had no skills in cooking or sewing or other domestic chores. She had no experience in anything a young woman is normally taught. She could play the piano like an angel and speak fluent French, over which he'd always marveled. She'd never been timid, never shied away from him…in fact she'd initiated and sought physical encounters.

She'd been a warm and enthusiastic bed partner.

No wonder she'd been so willing. No wonder she lacked restraint if she was no stranger to intimacies between men and women. He'd been so foolishly naive and blindly enamored that he'd imagined her desires were all because of her feelings for him.

Rita finally caught Lena by the arm and led her aside, where another woman joined them.

Paul went to Celeste, wrapping his arm around her supportively, and the two of them studied Nathan's reaction.

People on all sides spoke in hushed tones as he strode toward where Ella stood, her blue eyes wide and full of fear. He stared into those eyes and everything else faded into the background. He wanted her to tell him it wasn't so. He wanted it more than he wanted his next breath.

He couldn't bear for everything he believed about her to be a lie. Fixing her with a harsh stare, he demanded to know, "Is it true?"

Chapter Twenty

Ella stood trembling, but faced him. "Yes," she answered. "I was going to tell you."

He stared at her, his world collapsing inward. "What were you going to tell me?"

"The truth," she said. "All of it."

"And exactly what is the truth?" he asked.

The crowd had dispersed, many of them gathering their children and their belongings and heading for home. The musicians packed their instruments. Nathan and Ella were soon left standing alone.

"I was going to tell you that there never was a Miss Haversham's Academy for Young Women," she said. "We made that up after we saw the newspaper and decided to make a run for it. Celeste had already answered the ad. The rest of us joined up with her."

"And you weren't from Illinois."

She shook her head. "I grew up in Dodge City. In a parlor house run by Madame Fairchild."

"The first time we were together, you weren't a virgin."

She locked her gaze with his, and a heart-stopping moment passed before she said, "No."

The night air threatened to suffocate him. His chest hurt. Nathan turned toward the tent where his children were, vaguely aware of her behind him. He woke them, picking up Robby and taking Grace by the hand and setting off toward their street.

Christopher mumbled sleepy questions behind him, but Nathan didn't really hear them. Ella must have been back there, too, but he only turned once to make sure his son was keeping up.

A hundred confusing thoughts tumbled through his head, and Lena's words kept coming back to him. Accusations he'd expected his wife to deny. Expected someone to deny. Accusations he needed someone to deny.

She hadn't.

She'd looked at him like someone who'd had all their dirty laundry spilled out in public and who wanted to run the other way. She'd looked guilty.

He shifted Robby on his shoulder.

Mrs. Shippen heard them arrive and helped lead the children up the stairs. "Will you see them to bed?" he asked her.

"Yes, of course."

Without another word or acknowledging that Ella had

accompanied him home, he loped down the stairs and headed out the door, snapping it shut behind him.

Ella stared after Nathan. Her chest ached so badly, she couldn't draw a breath.

What had she done to him? It was bad enough she'd lied and hurt him, but she'd just destroyed his standing in the community and his political aspirations.

She stepped out onto the porch and stared into the darkness, wondering where he'd gone. He would come back. This was his home. His children were here. His life was here.

She was the one who would have to leave.

She stumbled to the top porch stair and lowered herself to a sitting position before she collapsed. She'd never wanted anything before. She'd never dared to hope for a future or a home or a family. Hope wasn't for women like her.

All the same she'd wanted to start fresh here.

She'd spent her youth and her young adulthood carefully guarding her mind and her heart from feeling anything...simply single-mindedly surviving the best she knew how. When Ansel had handed her that bankbook, she'd glimpsed a whole new world...and dared. Dared to leave Dodge behind and make a new life for herself.

She'd made friends. She'd discovered the joy of a family. She'd tasted freedom. She'd walked the streets of this town without ridicule or persecution.

She'd fallen in love.

She'd been utterly foolish.

Freedom and safety had been an illusion. Her weeks here had been merely a life based on deception. What had she imagined would happen? Had she thought no one would ever be the wiser?

Perhaps if she'd just smartened up and told Nathan sooner. Told him herself. Maybe he could have accepted the truth if it hadn't been thrown in his face in front of all of his friends and all the voters.

Ella's stomach lurched. She stood, ran down the stairs and around the side of the house and vomited behind the rosebushes. The looks on the people's faces earlier that evening swam before her eyes. Shock. Revulsion. Betrayal.

She had betrayed every person she'd met in Sweetwater, every person who'd shown kindness and extended friendship. She remembered the women talking about Bess Duncan in the mercantile and how they'd considered her unworthy of shopping in their stores.

When her stomach had settled and her knees were able to carry her back up the porch stairs, she entered the house. In the kitchen, she poured cool water into a pitcher and carried it upstairs. She'd been sleeping in Nathan's bed, but most of her things were still back in the space she now used mostly for a dressing room, so she closed herself into the first room she'd occupied upon her arrival. She removed her dress and washed up before donning a silk dressing gown and perching on the edge of the bed.

Wrapping her arms around herself, she considered how many people were affected by what Lena had done tonight. What were Rita and her liveryman husband doing at this moment? The other women and their situations crossed her mind.

The only relationship not in turmoil was Celeste and Paul's...because she'd told him the truth. Celeste wouldn't be welcomed back to the choir, however.

Ella thought of Betsy and Mildred and the other friends she'd made. She wouldn't be welcomed back to the choir, either. Or to church. Or the shops. She wouldn't be welcome period.

But what about Nathan? Would the citizens turn on him? Or would they understand he'd been as fooled as the rest of them?

Her chest hurt and her eyes burned. Wanting to disappear and escape this night, she curled up on the bed. She had nowhere to go.

Ella balled her fists, channeling her despair into anger directed at Lena for her hatefulness. Ella had never done anything to encourage the woman's loathing or jealousy, and such spitefulness was beyond her comprehension.

Her head ached. Regret and heartache consumed her. Her foolish hopes mocked her now. She wasn't worthy of Nathan. She would never be an asset to him or be held in esteem. Because of her past, she held no value whatsoever.

A hundred images and sounds flitted through her memory, snippets of days they'd spent together, things the children had said, moments she'd held so precious and dear...all part of the grand illusion—the world she'd fabricated out of lies and deception. None of it had actually been hers. None of it had been real.

She must have fallen asleep, because a soft knock at her door startled her. With a quick intake of breath, she sat up. "Come in."

Nathan entered, closing the door behind him and moving to stand at the foot of the bed.

Chapter Twenty-One

Her head still ached, and she worked to orient herself. The events of the evening came rushing back over Ella like a frigid tidal wave. She was thankful for the darkness that hid her shame, because she couldn't bear for him to look on her and she couldn't face the hurt in his eyes.

He wrapped a hand around the bedpost.

Her heart hammered.

"Is anyone looking for you?" he asked.

She rolled the question around in her head for a few seconds. "What do you mean?"

"Earlier you said that you and the other women decided to make a run for it. Meaning someone wanted to keep you in Dodge City? Meaning someone might not have been happy that you left?"

Ella held her gown tightly wrapped around her to calm her nerves. She knew how to tamp down emotion.

Distancing herself was how she'd survived for as long as she could remember. It had only been here—with this man, with his children—that she'd allowed herself to experience feelings, and now her lapse in judgment had come back to bite her. Hard.

"Madame Fairchild kept us in seclusion," she answered. "If we had any shopping to do, we were escorted."

She would tell him what she needed to say, and she would do so without a humiliating display. She took a deep breath. "We were told that the bars on the windows were for our protection, but we didn't have the option of leaving. We were Madame Fairchild's livelihood—and a pretty good one. We didn't see the money, of course. She handled all that and deducted our expenses."

Her mouth was dry, and she swallowed with difficulty. "But there's no way for her to learn where we are. Celeste got the train tickets secretively. Rita dosed the woman with laudanum, got the keys, and we sneaked out in the middle of the night. By the time she would have wakened the next day, we were long gone. Trains come and go from Dodge all the time, and we divided up so we wouldn't be noticed."

He stood without moving. Without speaking.

She thought back to his question. "So, no. No one is looking for us. For me. If I believed there was any possibility of drawing danger to your home or your children, I wouldn't be here."

"You deny nothing that Lena said this evening?"

Of course he wanted her to deny it. He didn't want to

believe he'd married a woman from a parlor house and brought her into his home. "I was going to tell you," she told him again. "I'd been thinking about it, but today I decided for certain. I just needed the opportunity."

"You decided today? Why was that?"

"Well…Celeste shared that she had told Paul. At first I was mortified, but then I realized that basing our marriage on lies was dishonorable, and you are an honorable man. You deserved the truth."

"And that never occurred to you *before* we were married? You never considered how that one detail might damage anything we could ever hope to build together?"

She deserved his anger. He was hurt. She'd done something inexcusable. "No."

"No?" he asked. "Just like that. No?"

"Would you have married me if you'd known?"

She couldn't make out his expression in the semidarkness, but he stood erect, still grasping the bedpost.

Nathan thought back to the night he'd met her. His fascination with and attraction to her had been overwhelming—and decidedly out of character. The council had encouraged him to take a wife to improve his chances of election, not destroy them. "No," he replied. "I wouldn't have."

"Well, there you have it," she said. "The whole point of pretending to have come from a young women's academy was to increase our chances for making marriages. It seemed like a good plan at the time. The only solution really."

He wanted to believe she'd been about to tell him the truth. But she hadn't been forthcoming. Now, after the fact, it was difficult to believe anything she said. Their marriage had been a lie. An act.

He was consumed with thoughts of her with other men. Countless other men, no doubt. She obviously took him for a complete fool, a besotted sop blinded by her beauty and charm and oblivious to all the signs that he should have been able to read.

Shouldn't he?

"You must have had a good laugh at my expense." At last some of the anger seeped into his words. "When I think of the way I've behaved around you, it makes me sick. My concern over your sensibilities. My reluctance to take you to my bed too soon for fear of souring you on the physical aspect of marriage. And you let me carry on. While all along you'd slept with a hundred men."

"It wasn't like that," she said. "And there were never a hundred men."

"I doubt you kept track."

"A tally wasn't necessary," she told him.

He would never sleep. How had she been able to fall into mindless slumber so easily? The fact that she had angered him further. He was too angry to hold a civil conversation. And he didn't want to wake the children.

"We'll talk tomorrow. Later today, rather." It was Sunday morning already. He wouldn't be going to church this day. The thought sickened him even more. He didn't want to face the reactions of his peers or the townspeople after last night's humiliating escapade.

"I'll leave," she told him. "Just give me time to pack my things, and I'll be out of here."

The thought was enough to send him into a panic, though for the life of him he didn't know why. "Where would you go?"

"I don't know, but I have funds. I can stay at the hotel. I'll buy a train ticket and be gone."

"To do what with yourself? Go back to Dodge City?"

"No. Never."

"Another city then. What kind of work could you find? Or would you be looking for another husband to take care of you?"

Her catch of breath was audible in the stillness of the shadowed room. He'd wounded her, but it didn't feel good. He didn't want to lash out. That's why he wanted to postpone conversation until he'd more tightly wrapped his anger.

"You have nowhere else to go. You will stay here while we work this out."

Work it out? Surely she was wondering what that meant, because he didn't have the faintest idea.

She said nothing. What could she say? He was right. He was the wronged party in this situation, and he darned well meant to have the final say in everything that happened from here on out. He was finished with being her play toy.

"I will ask Mrs. Shippen to take the children with her for the morning. You and I will talk then."

"Yes, of course," she answered meekly.

He turned and left her room then, pulling the door soundly shut. Silently, he entered the nursery and observed the children as they slept, oblivious to the unpleasantness that had entered their household and now threatened to shake things even more.

Tucking the sheet around Grace's shoulders, he pictured the way she looked at Ella. He remembered the excitement in his wife's voice when she spoke of Grace's conversations with the dolls. She might be a liar and a—he paused at even the thought of the word—prostitute, but she had made a difference in the lives of his children.

Anger welled anew, this time over the fact that she'd allowed his vulnerable offspring to grow attached to her. They'd experienced enough loss in their young lives without her thoughtless antics.

What was he thinking—that Ella would indeed leave? The prospect made his chest ache with dread. What if there was no other solution? Right now he couldn't think of one.

Nathan smoothed Christopher's hair, pressed his nose to Robby's cheek and kissed his forehead before leaving the nursery. In his room, he lit a lamp, removed his boots and shirt and washed in the tepid water left from earlier that evening.

Even after lying down, his brain wouldn't shut off. He thought of how Ella disliked being called beautiful. The fact that she found compliments offensive took on new meaning, and he tried to grasp the reasons behind her aversion. No doubt plenty of men had praised her beauty.

He remembered the jewelry she'd worn to dinner parties and while hosting their own gathering. It hadn't made sense that someone from a girl's academy possessed such lovely gems, but it made perfect sense for a high-class working woman to own them. The necklaces and earbobs might have been part of her wardrobe or she may have received them from her admirers.

He visualized the other women: Celeste, Rita, Lena.... While they were attractive, none were stunning beauties like Ella.

Gabrielle, he corrected himself. He'd heard that name several times now.

She must have been the most desirable woman in that parlor house. In that whole town for that matter.

The lamp was still burning, and Nathan studied the ceiling. He worked to picture Deborah, but his faded memories brought up the image in their photograph. She'd been pretty enough, with lustrous shining hair and a nice smile. His recollections brought to mind innocence and purity. Sometimes he'd felt as though his desire for her was a shameful thing. She'd never enjoyed intimacies, and had refused to discuss lovemaking or her aversion.

Ella, on the other hand, had been a willing and enthusiastic partner, showing preferences and inquiring of his. What man wouldn't have been delighted to have married a woman—not only exquisitely beautiful—but an unabashedly eager bed partner?

How many men had enjoyed those same delights?

Somehow he dozed for minutes or an hour and woke with thoughts of Paul Adams foremost in his aching head. Celeste had told the man and he'd carried on with being married to her—and obviously quite happily.

He dozed again and woke before dawn to dress and slip down the hallway. The door to the room where Mrs. Shippen slept when she stayed the night was already open, the bed neatly made, so he stole down the stairs.

He found the woman in the kitchen, drinking a cup of tea.

"I have a favor to ask of you this morning," he said, and then explained that he and Mrs. Lantry—his tongue tripped over the name—wouldn't be attending church. He would be grateful if she could take the children with her for the morning.

The woman was happy to oblige, and together they woke and dressed the three of them. Nathan hurried out to secure them a buggy before hugging and kissing each child and waving a goodbye.

Ella had heard the sounds of movement, signaling her that morning had arrived. A knock sounded at her door, and when she opened it, she found only a pitcher of warm water.

She washed and dressed in a green pinstriped skirt and a high-necked white blouse, shirred and edged with eyelet. She tied her hair back with a pair of trailing ribbons and added dainty earbobs.

Her eyes in the mirror lacked any sparkle, and her

skin seemed paler than normal, with a dark moon under each eye. She used rice powder in hopes of disguising her lack of sleep, but the result wasn't as effective as she'd hoped. What did it matter anyway? Her days here were numbered and her appearance made little difference.

At a rap on the door, she jumped and realized she'd been staring blindly into the mirror. She pressed her palms against her skirt and managed, "Come in."

The door opened and Nathan's broad form appeared from behind it. Her heart skittered nervously at the sight of him.

"The children are gone for the morning. Come have something to eat, and then we'll talk. You'll want a hat."

Where was he taking her? She hadn't packed. He'd told her she was staying here for now. Ella noticed the crystal atomizer in her hand and set it on the bureau. She joined Nathan where he waited in the hall, and at his gesture, led the way down the stairs and to the kitchen. Surely they weren't going to church.

Someone had prepared oatmeal, and he gestured for her to take a seat where a bowl sat.

He poured them both coffee and seated himself adjacent to her.

Ella picked up the spoon with fingers that trembled and took a bite of the warm cereal. There was nothing wrong with it, but she could barely swallow. She took another bite and forced it down. When she'd consumed half the bowlful, she set down the utensil, dabbed her lips with a napkin and reached for the coffee.

It was hot and strong, and he had sweetened hers the way she preferred it. She wondered if he could hear her heart beating as loudly as she could.

She dared look at him. He studied her with furrowed brows, just as she'd sensed. She'd felt his sharp gaze on her. His expression wasn't angry or even repulsed as she'd expected. Instead, when their eyes met, she recognized the hurt of betrayal.

Apologies stuck in her throat. Nothing she could say would make a difference now.

Chapter Twenty-Two

"Are you finished eating?"

"Ye—" She cleared her throat. "Yes, thank you."

He cleared away the dishes without washing them, then picked up her hat and gestured to the back door.

She took her hat and opened the door, crossing the back porch to unlock the screen door. One after the other, they stepped out into the sunshine.

It was difficult to believe the beauty of this slope of land remained untouched and green with life when everything else had been tumbled about and sullied. Nathan took the lead and strolled toward the stream. His pace indicated no rush. It seemed as though they were simply out for a morning walk to enjoy the weather and each other's company.

Once they'd reached the bank, now riotously blooming with tiny blue flowers and white-tipped pink clover, he halted and stood facing the gurgling water.

Ella remembered the first time they'd come here and how she'd waded into the water and lost her balance. She thought of the two of them floundering in the cold water—and how she'd impetuously kissed him for the first time.

Was he remembering, too? She wanted to look at him, but stared instead at the sparkling surface.

Beside her he moved and seated himself on the ground. She took her cue, moving to sit several feet away.

Silence stretched between them until a bird broke it by twittering from a nearby branch. Another bird answered in kind. Mates perhaps.

"I know it's far too late," she said, automatically smoothing her green skirt and then forcing her hand to lie still. "And you have every reason to be angry. And disappointed."

He made a low noise in his throat, drawing her gaze to his face.

"*Disappointed* isn't a strong enough word, of course. You have every right to be furious with me. I deceived you, you and everyone else. I pretended to be someone who would fit into your life and make you a good wife."

He glanced away for a brief moment, but then drew his gaze back to her face.

"At the time I didn't see any other way," she told him. "I'd never been on my own, never learned any skills, didn't know how to earn a living."

He was probably considering the same thing she was

at that moment—thinking about her skills for earning a living. For the first time she could remember, her face grew uncomfortably warm with embarrassment—or more likely shame.

"And then one evening Celeste came to my room. Her eye was just healing from the previous weekend."

"What happened the previous weekend?" he asked at last.

"One of the young cowboys who preferred her company would drink too much before—and while—visiting her on Saturday nights. But as long as he presented himself well at dinner and was clean and mannerly while in Madame Fairchild's presence, he was allowed to accompany Celeste to her room. Once there, he promptly pulled out a hidden flask. As the evening progressed he became aggressive. Sometimes, if he grew loud, he'd be tossed out, but he was always allowed back."

"Because he could pay for her time."

"Yes, and it was most likely his entire wages."

"So the night Celeste came to your room," he prompted.

"She had clipped a notice from the newspaper. The one the men from Sweetwater had posted, regarding your need for young, intelligent, refined maidens of a loving disposition for the purpose of matrimony," she quoted.

"In hindsight perhaps we weren't specific enough," he remarked, rather unkindly.

She directed her gaze to her hands in her lap while she regained her composure.

"Go on," he said without apology.

She glanced up into the branches of the trees that lined the stream, seeking the birds that were now calling back and forth to each other. One flew from its hiding place and swooped down to the grass, where it plucked a worm from the earth.

"I had just received notice from my gentleman caller that he was moving away. Back East, he said." She hadn't mentioned that was where his wife wanted to go. But then Ella caught herself withholding the truth because it wasn't pretty, and exposed it with her next breath. "His sons were off to university, and his wife wished to move back to be near her family."

She turned her gaze upon Nathan. He still watched her, but said nothing.

"No money was ever exchanged between the gentlemen and the women. That would have appeared too gauche for Madame Fairchild, who liked the appearance of manners and civility and propriety. There were rules of conduct we had to follow. But that particular night my gentleman caller—"

"You make it sound as though he was courting you."

She nodded. "That's the way we learned to speak of our duties. That evening he gave me a bankbook with a balance that took my breath away. He was a very kind and thoughtful man."

Nathan tightened his jaw, but he said nothing.

"He advised me to leave Dodge while I still could. His warnings mirrored my fears of growing older and being forced to survive in…well, unpleasant conditions." She swallowed because she had never spoken of this. "That's what happened to my mother. She wasn't old when she died. She simply didn't want to live such a hard life any longer."

"What happened to her?"

"The women no longer young and those not considered beautiful have a more difficult time," she explained.

"How did you come to be at Madame Fairchild's in the first place?"

"Most likely I was born there," she answered. "I can't remember anything else."

Nathan heard her explanation, but it took a full minute for the concept to settle into his mind. Born in a whore-house? His thoughts immediately raced to his children and the way they'd been protected and cosseted and shielded from every unpleasant thing.

He remembered Ella's reaction upon meeting his children and learning of their daily routine. Everything about Sweetwater, about his life and family had been a foreign experience. And he thought back to how she'd wanted to take them to see the acrobats, and how she'd enjoyed the day as much as they had.

He tried to imagine her upbringing. "What was it like?" he asked finally, unable to wonder any longer.

"I always had my own room. Tutors were provided. I had books and nice clothing and good food."

"What about friends?"

"There were no other children. I saw my mother on Sundays, until she died that is. I was nine, I believe."

She'd been groomed for her position. Groomed by a

heartless woman who saw a beautiful child as a commodity. The thought sickened him. He experienced fear on her behalf. "What about men?" he asked, then clarified, "Customers?"

Ella brushed nonexistent lint from her skirt. "I didn't have a gentleman caller until I was seventeen."

Nathan's tense jaw and body relaxed a measure.

"Although I was coached and occasionally I watched."

He swallowed hard and took a deep breath.

"Once I was old enough, I learned that Ansel had been waiting for me. He was always kind and thoughtful," she told him. "Even then."

Nathan's gut twisted. "The same man that gave you the bankbook?"

She nodded. "Even then he was considerate. I was almost able to pretend I had a life like the characters in the books I read, except I had no choice in the matter, of course."

"You were a prisoner," he said.

"A pet," she pointed out and turned her face away. "When I first came here I felt as free as these birds."

Of course she had. The wide-eyed enjoyment she showed over discoveries of the most simple things made perfect sense now. If what she said was true, she'd had no choice about her upbringing or her position before running away and coming here.

But that didn't change the fact that she'd married him under less-than-scrupulous conditions.

Earlier she'd said she'd pretended to be someone she

wasn't in order to fit in and make him a good wife, and her words had stuck in his craw. She had fit into his life perfectly and made him an excellent wife, that made this turn of events all the more confusing and difficult to sort through.

Hearing her speak of this Ansel fellow was more than he could cope with at the moment. Even if she'd been raised into that life and knew nothing else, it didn't hurt him any less to think of it now.

He had a compulsive need to know details that could only wound him. "You said last night that there weren't a hundred men."

"That's correct."

If she wasn't forthcoming, he'd have to ask. He took a breath. "Can you make a guess at how many?"

"I don't need to guess. I know."

He turned then and found her looking at him as though she'd been waiting for him to meet her eyes.

She was as lovely as she'd always been, incredibly beautiful, though she didn't like the word or the reminder. He wondered briefly now why that was. Obviously it had something to do with her feelings of value—or lack of.

Her chaste white blouse and pale coloring gave her the deceivingly youthful appearance of innocence.

"You were the second, Nathan. There was only one other."

At last he was able to release a breath and ask, "How can that be?"

"Because he was extremely wealthy and able to afford

my exclusive attentions. He secured me for himself, enabling me to have only a sole gentleman caller. I was extremely fortunate."

Everything was relative, depending on one's background and experiences, he thought. The fact that she considered being someone's pet fortunate only pointed out how much worse her situation might have been—and how much worse those of the other women most likely had been.

But she'd done an excellent job of deception the first time. He had no reason to believe she couldn't do it again to secure her home. "Fool me once, shame on you. Fool me twice, shame on me."

Of course she couldn't expect him to believe her. Ella folded her hands in her lap and turned her head to watch the sparkling stream from beneath the brim of her straw hat. He would most likely divorce her. She'd be unable to get a job in this town—no one would hire her. Even if someone did give her employment, she'd be unable to face the ridicule and scornful looks.

"I regret hurting you," she said at last. "And the children."

"They don't know," he said.

"They will. Christopher goes to school. Parents will talk." At that moment, with thoughts of how the children would suffer because of her, she closed off. Shut down. Not feeling was what she did best.

Willing her face, body and mind into complete composure, she discovered a squirrel digging at the base of a tree, most likely searching for an acorn he'd buried the previous fall. She envied the animal its mindless pursuit of food, without concern for relationships or opinions.

She wouldn't think about leaving the children behind—about saying goodbye. She would assess her finances, pack and rent a room at the hotel. While staying there, she would buy a newspaper and see if there was a position available in a nearby town—or even a town far away. At this point it didn't matter where she went.

Nathan had spoken, but she didn't hear his words. She stood and made her way up the grassy slope to the house. The sooner she cut herself off from him and this place, the better.

Chapter Twenty-Three

Nathan had dressed in trousers and a plain cotton shirt, the sleeves rolled back and collar open in deference to the sunny morning. Saddling a horse from the livery, he rode to the Adams place, enjoying something he seldom took time to do anymore.

After their conversation the day before, Ella hadn't left her room the rest of the day or that evening, even when the children returned. Before leaving this morning, he'd asked Mrs. Shippen to take her a tray of food.

Dismounting at the gate that opened into a dooryard of mostly dirt and pecking chickens, he tied the horse and glanced around.

The door opened, and Celeste exited the tiny dwelling. She had cut her hair, so that it was only two inches long all over her head, and the remaining waves were a bright orange-red in the sunlight. The tresses had a tendency to curl and formed a shining cap upon her head. He found the look surprisingly attractive, and much of that was due to the air of confidence and peace she'd adopted over the few weeks he'd known her. Right now she appeared puzzled at seeing him.

"Mr. Lantry," she said, wiping her hands on her apron. "What brings you out here alone?"

"I was hoping to talk to Paul," Nathan told her.

"I think he's mending fences to the west." She shaded her eyes and gazed in that direction. "I won't see him until noon."

"Thank you." Nathan reached for the reins to untie the horse.

"How is Ella?"

"She hasn't come out of her room."

"May I call on her?"

He nodded. "Yes, of course."

He touched the brim of his hat in a polite farewell and mounted the horse. Paul wasn't difficult to find. Nathan followed the line of freshly repaired fencing until he spotted the man.

Paul bent over a post, wrapping wire in place. At Nathan's approach, he straightened and tipped his hat back on his head. He took a red kerchief from the rear pocket of his overalls and wiped his face. "What brings you out here, Nathan?"

Nathan got down, still holding the reins. He walked toward the other man. "I was hoping we could talk."

Paul studied him briefly, then turned and pointed to a stand of willows. "How about in the shade?"

Nathan led the horse beneath the branches and

tethered him to a low branch, where he could crop grass. A saddlebag nearby indicated Paul had already been using this spot for his breaks.

Paul lowered himself to the clover and sat holding his hat, his wrists draped over his bent knees. He waited for Nathan to speak.

Nathan cleared his throat. "Ella said you already knew about Madame Fairchild and Dodge City before Lena told the entire county."

Paul nodded. "Celeste told me."

"Why do you think she told you?"

He appeared to consider the question. "A lie is a burdensome thing. I think she didn't want to carry it around anymore."

"How did you…? How were you able to accept the truth? Did it change things? Did it…cause you pain?"

Paul gazed out across his land before looking back at Nathan. "It's easy to get comfortable in our narrow little worlds," he said finally. "Sometimes we forget just how hard life is beyond this place we've created. Females without fathers or husbands to look out for 'em have a rough time of it.

"Celeste's daddy sold her off when she was no more 'n a girl. He thought the fellow was gonna marry her, but instead he dragged her 'n a couple other girls in and out of the railroad camps, where they lived in tents. They cooked, washed 'n whored for the men who built the rails.

"When Celeste got away from that man, working

at that parlor house in Dodge City seemed like a fair-weather picnic. Besides, it was all she knew how to do."

He looked directly at Nathan then. "It don't matter none to me what she did before. She didn't choose that life. She didn't have no choice but to survive any way she could. She survived, and she's here now. She's a good person with a big heart for love."

Nathan let the other man's words sink in. It was plain he loved the wild-haired woman he'd married. He overlooked her background because he loved her.

This was all the more difficult for Nathan because he had fallen in love with Ella. Because he'd trusted her and now felt betrayed. "What about the lie?" he asked. "Doesn't it bother you that she deceived you in order to get married?"

"It did at first, to be sure. But then I thought about what I would have done if it had been me an' I'd needed a way out of that life. The frontier is mostly about starting over," he added. "My pa robbed his share o' trains in his day. Then he had a family and settled down to raise us. He was a good man and brought up his sons to obey the law. People change."

Nathan studied him. "I never knew that."

"All the people in Sweetwater have a past," Paul said with a shrug. "Some good, some bad. Seems to me a person is who they turn out to be, not who they were before."

"But…" Nathan took off his hat and turned it by the brim in his hands, without looking at Paul. "How do you reconcile thinking of her with those men? That happened."

Paul took a jar from the saddlebag. He unscrewed the lid and offered it to Nathan. "Lemonade?" At Nathan's polite refusal, he took a long drink and screwed the lid back on. "Celeste's with me now because she wants to be. And because she has a choice. She chose me."

Nathan threaded a hand into his hair.

"She's past that," Paul said. "If you love Ella...if you still want her for your wife, you have to move out of your own way."

Nathan looked at him then.

Paul's eyes were bright in his sun-darkened face. "Don't let pride stand in the way of what you might have."

Anger stabbed Nathan. Pride? That was fine for Paul to say. His career wasn't dangling in the balance.

Immediately, he corrected himself. Paul had just as much, if not more, to let go of than Nathan, and he'd done so. And he appeared happy and quite content.

Celeste had, however, come to him with the truth herself. Nathan wondered how much of a difference that would have made for him if Ella had been forthcoming before it was too late.

They sat for a while longer, and the subject turned to the weather and the summer wheat. Finally, Nathan stretched to his full height, shook hands with the other man and took his leave.

The rest of that day and the next passed with his mind in turmoil. When he went to work, his presence drew a few stares on the street, and the man who worked for him, taking care of paperwork inquired only about business matters. Everyone knew he'd been made a fool of, but so far no one had spoken of it.

Ella had come to supper, but she'd been silent, eating as though waiting for something to happen. Perhaps she waited for him to address the subject...or for him to ask her to pack and leave.

Fortunately, the children hadn't been exposed to the unpleasantness and therefore went about their days and evenings as though nothing had changed.

"Will you read to us tonight?" Christopher asked as they finished their meal.

Nathan glanced up to see his son had directed the question to him. He nodded. "Yes, of course."

They settled in his study, with all three youngsters piling around him on the divan.

Grace stretched both arms toward Ella, indicating she wanted her to hold her and join them.

Nathan nodded at her.

She picked up the child and seated herself beside Nathan, without allowing their arms to touch.

Nathan read aloud, and the children quieted. Sometime later, he glanced over to see his daughter snuggled into Ella's lap. Even though Robby sat on his lap, he had reached for and held her hand.

His children had already grown to love and depend on her.

Later, as they tucked them into bed, his chest ached with unexpressed emotions. Grace picked up the rag doll

Ella had tucked in beside her and spoke to it. "What? You want Momma to give you a hug and a kiss? Okay."

She turned the doll's cloth face up toward Ella.

He didn't know who was more surprised, him or Ella. But she very calmly leaned down and gave the doll a hug and a kiss. "Good night, Dolly," she said. "You're a very special little dolly, and I love you."

Grace had referred to Ella as Momma. He could hardly draw a breath. He understood now the parallel that Ella drew between herself and these children. She had never known the love or protection they took for granted, but instead of resenting them for it, she was appreciative and protective.

As he kissed his daughter good-night, he considered what it had been like for a child like her to grow up in a gilded cage with no say in her future. If his precious innocent daughter had been placed into the same circumstances, she wouldn't be evil or immoral. She would be a survivor.

Truth be told, Ella had been innocent. She was innocent. By no desire of her own had she been ensconced in that lifestyle and rented out to that man like a buggy he took for a Sunday drive.

They left the room and stood in the light cast by the hissing gas lamp on the hallway wall. She was the most beautiful woman he'd ever laid eyes on. He missed having her beside him at night. He missed taking her in his arms, knowing her warm willing kisses and the pleasure of her body.

The sheen of tears in her eyes caught him by surprise. "Why are you crying?"

"You heard her," she said. "What she called me." She fumbled with her sleeve, withdrew a lacy handkerchief and blotted her eyes. "I never meant for them to be hurt, Nathan. You have to believe that."

"I do," he relented. He touched his knuckle to her chin and raised her face. "I don't believe you wanted to hurt anyone."

She raised the hand that clenched the hankie to his chest and took a tiny step forward.

He took a step as well, and she was in his arms, as soft and warm as he remembered and smelling of cinnamon and musk. His body reacted as it always did at her scent and her nearness, blurring everything else and bringing his need for her into sharp awareness.

He lowered his head and kissed her deeply, his tongue searching for hers. She responded in kind, with a heady intake of breath that brought her breasts up against him.

He swept her up easily, and she wrapped her arms around his neck and held on tightly. In several strides, he reached the door to his room, kicked it open and strode ahead to lay her on the bed.

She reached for his jacket, tugging it away, followed by his shirt, which he helped her remove. He urged her to roll facing away so he could unfasten her dress. Tugging the fabric downward, he met resistance where she lay on it and urged her up, so he could remove the garment and toss it aside.

Within seconds, he'd divested her of her corset, her chemise and pantaloons, and rubbed the wrinkled skin of her sides and belly in the manner that made her purr and wrap herself around him.

He remained standing beside the bed, and she got up on her knees to frame his face with both hands and kiss him. He was weak where she was concerned. He couldn't resist her, had never been able to deny this passionate desire that burned between them and consumed them both.

The thought of her with that other man drove him crazy. The thought of that man with his hands on her ate at him like acid. He wanted to obliterate anyone else from her mind—from her past, from her experience. He was greedy for her, selfish with need. Hell-bent to possess her.

He released her to free his hands so he could kick off his shoes and tug off his trousers, and then he pushed her back on the bed. She reached for him, touching him until he shuddered. His skin tightened and his pulse roared in his ears. This mindless need for her was crazy and all consuming.

Nothing could have stopped him from raking his tongue across her skin until she whimpered. He teased her with just enough pleasure to make her entire body tense in rigid anticipation of more…and then let the sensations abate while he moved his attentions elsewhere.

"Nathan," she said at last, her voice gravelly with desire. "Nathan, come to me now."

He held himself above her, pinning her in place with

his gaze, then brought his knee up and ground it against her until she gasped. She pulled him to her. He buried himself, rocked against her, hard.

He loved her still, loved her as he'd never loved before. He couldn't imagine a lifetime without her. She was his wife now, and as necessary to his existence as breathing.

She let out a soft cry and shuddered against him, and he followed her into blissful release.

Nathan rolled to his side and cupped her face to look into her eyes. He kissed her and held her close, their arms and legs entwined. He didn't know how, but he knew he had to get out of his own way, as Paul had advised him.

Pride and inflexibility would be his downfall if he didn't learn how to unselfishly love and forgive her.

Most of his shame and anger stemmed from the fact that he'd always felt out of control with her. He'd succumbed to his desire for her like a witless fool. She made him feel alive. Made him feel like a man. And the fact had embarrassed him, as though he considered himself above those kinds of emotions—and shameless devotion.

"Ella?" he said softly.

She didn't respond.

"I'm used to being in control," he said. "All I know how to do is keep things neat and tidy and adhere to a code of ethics. I expect too much, I know. I'm inflexible."

He kissed her smooth, cool forehead.

"I'm tired of keeping everything in balance," he confessed. "And I don't know what to do when circumstances are beyond my control. I don't like the feeling."

She had fallen asleep, but he tested the words on the air. "I feel out of control with you, and that scares me. But I like it, too."

He smoothed her hair over her shoulder. "I'm sad for the child you never got to be," he whispered.

Minutes later, sleep overtook him.

Nathan woke and opened his eyes.

The house was silent. The bed beside him was empty.

He sat and took his bearings, getting up to wash and dress. He checked the time before tucking his pocket watch away. He'd never before been late to work that he could recall. Why had Ella let him sleep so long?

Light streamed from inside the room Ella had used previously, creating a lopsided rectangle on the wooden floor. He glanced in and stopped in his tracks.

Backing up, he walked in and took inventory of each bare surface, then opened drawers and finally the armoire.

Nothing. The room sat as empty as when she'd first arrived.

Ella was gone.

Chapter Twenty-Four

He doubled-checked to be sure—though he couldn't have overlooked the amount of clothing she owned—but no, none of her belongings had been moved to his room.

She'd packed them.

With a jolt of alarm, he charged out of his room and took the stairs two at a time, then searched the bottom floor. Grace and Robby were playing on the back porch, while Charlotte peeled potatoes.

"Where is everyone?" he asked the woman.

"I took Christopher to school. Mrs. Shippen has gone to the market."

"And my wife?" he demanded.

"Mrs. Lantry left quite early," she told him.

"How did she get all of her belongings out without my knowledge?"

"They were picked up yesterday," she explained.

"By whom?"

"I don't know, sir. My guess is Pete Driscoll."

She was gone. Had Ella boarded a train that morning? What was she thinking and planning? Nathan greeted Grace and Robby with a brief kiss, before hurrying back through the house. He grabbed his hat from the rack near the front door and half ran the distance to Main Street, where he entered the livery.

Pete sat on a barrel, cleaning a harness, smoke from a pipe curling around his head. An orange-striped cat rubbed its arched back against his pant leg.

"Pete!"

"Mornin', Mr. Lantry. Need a driver today?"

"Not presently," he replied. "Did you haul my wife's trunks yesterday?"

"Yes, sir. Mrs. Lantry had a passel o' stuff she needed moved. The Parker lad helped me. Has a strong back, he does."

"Where did you take her things? To the train station?"

"No, sir. The hotel. Third floor, as luck would have it."

The hotel? Nathan turned and shot out the door, heading for the brick building down the street. A carriage was parked at the curb, and a man helped a woman down to the boardwalk. Nathan dodged around them to enter the building.

He didn't recognize the fellow at the front desk, but the man knew him by name. "Good morning, Mr. Lantry. How may I help you?"

"Which room is my wife in?"

He checked his ledger and looked up. "Three-twelve."

Nathan turned toward the stairs, but the man's voice halted him. "But she's not there."

Nathan turned back. Was he too late? He rested a palm on the counter and raised his eyebrows in impatience.

"She's in the dining room," the man explained, gesturing to a wide hallway that led away from the lobby. "Back there."

"Thank you." Nathan remembered to take off his hat and carried it as he jogged along the carpeted hallway, the sounds of clanking dishes and tinkling silverware growing louder as he approached.

Half a dozen tables were filled with couples and families, but at one near a side window, Ella sat alone.

His heart kicked in his chest at the sight of her.

At his approach, she glanced up in surprise, and let her tea cup clank against its saucer. "Nathan!"

He stood awkwardly beside the table for only a moment, and then slid onto the chair across from her. "What are you doing here?"

Her cheeks were bright pink, and she didn't meet his gaze, but studied the handle of a butter knife as though it fascinated her. "I sent a letter of apology to the territorial board of directors. I apologized for my deceit and requested they absolve you from any knowledge or responsibility. I asked them to consider that you had no knowledge of where I'd come from—or where any of the girls had come from for that matter—just as none of the town council knew. You shouldn't be looked upon unfavorably when they consider placing their support behind you in the election, and I told them so."

She raised her regretful blue gaze to his. "It's my greatest wish that they will place the blame where it lies, and not upon your shoulders. I couldn't bear to be the reason you weren't considered as a candidate."

"What about last night?" he asked. "Did that mean nothing to you?"

"It meant everything to me," she replied. "You and your children mean everything to me. Because of that I don't want to cause them hurt, nor do I want to stand in the way of your career."

"If you don't want to hurt us, then don't leave. I'd be only half a man if I didn't ask your forgiveness and beg you to stay."

"What on earth have you done that begs my forgiveness?" she asked. "I'm the one who deceived you."

"I was so concerned with being in control." He reached for her hand. "I let pride get in the way of love and forgiveness. I was embarrassed that people in town knew I'd been duped, but that was so superficial. I really don't care what people think of me...or of you for that matter. I care what *you* think of me, and I pray you don't think I'm selfish or prideful."

"Of course not. You're kind and generous."

"That's what you said about your gentleman friend," he pointed out. "And I was jealous."

"He *was* kind," she answered. "And I appreciated that.

But I never loved him." Her chin quivered. "I love you, Nathan."

"And I love you, Ella. Say you'll stay here and be my wife for as long as we live."

"But your position. I would be an encumbrance."

"I'll withdraw my name from consideration. Being the governor would be a shallow victory if it meant being without you."

"You're talking about giving up your career."

"I'm also the city attorney," he said, "and I haven't broken my contract. Besides I have any number of interests that can see me through. I own a furniture store and a lumberyard. I can refocus my interests in the blink of an eye."

"You own a furniture store?"

He nodded.

"Was it the one where I shopped?"

He shook his head.

She covered her lips with her fingers. "Oh, my."

"The fact that you bought furniture elsewhere for our home pointed out that we need to stay abreast of the items women would like to see in stock. You shopped at the other place because of availability."

"And quality."

"Noted," he said with a wry nod. "Perhaps you'll help select stock in the future."

Hearing him speak of the future gave Ella hope, but filled her with regret at the same time. She didn't want to be the reason Nathan missed out on any of his dreams. She understood the true nature of people, and no matter how much she improved or changed, the difference would never be enough to make all of them forgive. And they could never forget.

Nathan reached for her other hand, taking her trembling cold fingers into his warm steady grasp. "You never had anyone to love you or look out for you," he said in a gruff low voice. "You have been all alone in this world, doing the best you knew how. You never had an example of family, and you never had a choice but to do what was expected of you.

"You have a choice today, Ella. I will never hold you where you don't want to be, and I won't try to manipulate your feelings. If you choose to stay in Sweetwater and be my wife, I want it to be because you love me and for no other reason than because you want to be here."

Tears blurred her vision, and she blinked them away, but she shook her head. "I don't deserve your love."

Nathan glanced aside, as though noting what the diners were doing. Ella looked, too, but the nearby tables were empty and no one at any other table was paying any attention to them. "That's where you're wrong," he said when he looked back. "You deserve to be loved as much as anyone else. You deserve love as much as you believe Grace deserves love and attention," he said, as though he knew those words would reach her heart.

"You deserve a family and a fresh start," he assured her.

"But everyone knows…"

"Ella," he said sternly and leveled his intense gaze. "It doesn't matter what anyone else knows or thinks. I would give up my career if need be, but it won't be necessary. I would move away if it meant we'd be together."

Her eyes prickled with tears.

"You can't change your past. None of us can. But we can build a future. Together."

The knowledge that he loved her and wanted her filled her heart and soothed aches that had been open wounds for as long as she could remember. Nathan couldn't change her past, but knowing him—loving him, being his wife—would change her future, and she loved the sound of that promise.

"What do you say?" he asked, his eyes alight with hope. "Will you stay and be my wife?"

There was nothing she wanted more. "Yes," she answered. "I will."

At the next meeting of the territorial board of directors, Nathan was asked to wait in the corridor outside the boardroom at city hall while a discussion ensued. He'd already resolved that any decision would sit well with him. He had other avenues if politics weren't in his future.

The heavy oak door opened. "Will you join us, please?" Carl Lawrence asked and stepped aside for Nathan to enter.

Nathan couldn't tell by the expressions of the dozen men what their verdict had been, but he seated himself in preparation.

Tall silver-haired Mayor Simpson of Sweetwater took the floor as the spokesperson. "Nathan," he began. "The council considers itself largely responsible for the recent unfortunate misunderstanding."

Nathan glanced at the faces around the table.

"It was this very council, after all, that came up with the plan to send for women, particularly in the hope that a wife would improve your family image. We had good intentions." The mayor glanced at his fellow business-men, who nodded in agreement.

"Several of our friends and neighbors have married because of that plan, yourself included."

Nathan glanced at Henry Thomas, who had married Rita. Henry met his gaze without looking away.

"This wasn't a difficult decision," the mayor contin-ued. "We're of a mind that these women traveled here to start over. The frontier is about starting over," he added, and Nathan thought about what Paul had told him about his own father. Few people didn't have something in their past they wanted to forget.

"In conversation with the townspeople and business owners, even with Reverend Kane, we believe these women's true pasts won't be mentioned again—and the knowledge about where they came from will definitely not pass outside Sweetwater's city limits.

"Nathan, you are our choice for governor of the Ter-ritory of Wyoming."

Nathan let his gaze travel from face to face, seeing agreement, approval and friendship. "Thank you," he said. "I was prepared to turn my interests in another direction, to be honest. But since you've chosen me for this job—and I have your trust and support—I will be proud to represent the people of the territory."

A brief business meeting followed, during which Nathan impatiently participated, but couldn't wait to get home and let Ella know the news.

Dressed in a cornflower-blue skirt and a white pin-striped shirtwaist, she met him on the front porch. Her blue eyes were bright with questions.

"I'm the candidate," he told her. And then he explained how the board had decided never to speak of where Ella or any of the other women had come from. Sweetwater would erase that information. The women who'd come from Dodge would be accepted the same as everyone else from this time forward.

"Someday the children might hear of it," Ella said.

"And if so, they'll understand acceptance, and forgiveness and love as a way of life," he told her.

She took his hand and led him to a padded wicker love seat that hadn't been on the porch before.

"Where did this come from?" he asked.

She urged him to sit and snuggled beside him. "They're carrying them at your store now. There's a whole selection of porch furniture."

He chuckled.

The screen opened and Grace joined them, leading Robby by the hand. "Don't cry, Robby," Grace said. "Momma will hold you and kiss your finger."

He held his index finger up to Ella. Tears shone in his round eyes. "Kiss."

Ella shot Nathan a look of surprise. Grace had spoken

to her little brother! She reached to pull him onto her lap, kissed his finger and snuggled him.

Nathan pulled Grace onto his knees. "So, Miss Grace. You talk to your doll and you talk to Robby. Does that mean you're going to be talking to us now?"

She gave him a bashful look from the corner of her eye and nodded.

"What will you say when you talk to us?" he asked.

She stuck a finger in her mouth and shrugged.

"Maybe she'll ask for liver and onions for supper," Ella suggested.

Grace shook her head and grimaced around her finger.

"Maybe she'll ask if she can help Charlotte clean the ashes out of the stove," Nathan said.

Grace rolled her eyes and giggled, pulling her finger away. "No, I will not."

Nathan grinned. "What will you say, then?" he asked.

"I will say I want to pway the piano wiff Momma."

Nathan hugged her and kissed her cheek. Ella and Robby hugged her, too.

The screen opened again and Christopher joined them. "What's everybody looking so happy about?"

"We're just happy to be a family," Nathan told him.

"Let's go play the piano," Ella said with a smile.

The younger children jumped down and headed for the door, joined by their older brother. Nathan caught Ella's hand and held her back for a kiss. "Thank you."

"For what?" she asked, skimming her hand along his jaw and looking into his eyes.

"For marrying me."

"It was my pleasure, Mr. Lantry. Thank you for loving me."

"That was *my* pleasure," he assured her.

"Are you kissing *again?*" Christopher called.

The couple entered the house, and in moments the flawless notes of a Bach concerto floated on the summer air, joined by the discordant rasps of a harmonica and the gleeful sound of laughter.

* * * * *

COMING NEXT MONTH FROM

HARLEQUIN®
HISTORICAL

Available July 26, 2011

- **THE GUNFIGHTER AND THE HEIRESS**
  by **Carol Finch**
  (Western)

- **PRACTICAL WIDOW TO PASSIONATE MISTRESS**
  by **Louise Allen**
  (Regency)
  (First in *The Transformation of the Shelley Sisters* trilogy)

- **THE GOVERNESS AND THE SHEIKH**
  by **Marguerite Kaye**
  (Regency)
  (Second in *Princes of the Desert* duet)

- **SEDUCED BY HER HIGHLAND WARRIOR**
  by **Michelle Willingham**
  (Medieval)
  (Second in *The MacKinloch Clan* family saga)

You can find more information on upcoming
Harlequin® titles, free excerpts and more at
www.HarlequinInsideRomance.com.

REQUEST YOUR FREE BOOKS!

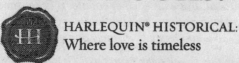

HARLEQUIN® HISTORICAL:
Where love is timeless

2 FREE NOVELS PLUS 2 FREE GIFTS!

YES! Please send me 2 FREE Harlequin® Historical novels and my 2 FREE gifts (gifts are worth about $10). After receiving them, if I don't wish to receive any more books, I can return the shipping statement marked "cancel." If I don't cancel, I will receive 6 brand-new novels every month and be billed just $5.19 per book in the U.S. or $5.74 per book in Canada. That's a savings of at least 17% off the cover price! It's quite a bargain! Shipping and handling is just 50¢ per book in the U.S. and 75¢ per book in Canada.* I understand that accepting the 2 free books and gifts places me under no obligation to buy anything. I can always return a shipment and cancel at any time. Even if I never buy another book, the two free books and gifts are mine to keep forever.

246/349 HDN FEQQ

Name	(PLEASE PRINT)	

Address		Apt. #

City	State/Prov.	Zip/Postal Code

Signature (if under 18, a parent or guardian must sign)

Mail to the Reader Service:
IN U.S.A.: P.O. Box 1867, Buffalo, NY 14240-1867
IN CANADA: P.O. Box 609, Fort Erie, Ontario L2A 5X3

Not valid for current subscribers to Harlequin Historical books.

Want to try two free books from another line?
Call 1-800-873-8635 or visit www.ReaderService.com.

* Terms and prices subject to change without notice. Prices do not include applicable taxes. Sales tax applicable in N.Y. Canadian residents will be charged applicable taxes. Offer not valid in Quebec. This offer is limited to one order per household. All orders subject to credit approval. Credit or debit balances in a customer's account(s) may be offset by any other outstanding balance owed by or to the customer. Please allow 4 to 6 weeks for delivery. Offer available while quantities last.

Your Privacy—The Reader Service is committed to protecting your privacy. Our Privacy Policy is available online at www.ReaderService.com or upon request from the Reader Service.

We make a portion of our mailing list available to reputable third parties that offer products we believe may interest you. If you prefer that we not exchange your name with third parties, or if you wish to clarify or modify your communication preferences, please visit us at www.ReaderService.com/consumerchoice or write to us at Reader Service Preference Service, P.O. Box 9062, Buffalo, NY 14269. Include your complete name and address.

HH11B

Once bitten, twice shy. That's Gabby Wade's motto—
especially when it comes to Adamson men.
And the moment she meets Jon Adamson her theory
is confirmed. But with each encounter a little something
sparks between them, making her wonder if she's been
too hasty to dismiss this one!

Enjoy this sneak peek from ONE GOOD REASON
by Sarah Mayberry, available August 2011
from Harlequin® Superromance®.

Gabby Wade's heartbeat thumped in her ears as she marched to her office. She wanted to pretend it was because of her brisk pace returning from the file room, but she wasn't that good a liar.

Her heart was beating like a tom-tom because Jon Adamson had touched her. In a very male, very possessive way. She could still feel the heat of his big hand burning through the seat of her khakis as he'd steadied her on the ladder.

It had taken every ounce of self-control to tell him to unhand her. What she'd really wanted was to grab him by his shirt and, well, explore all those urges his touch had instantly brought to life.

While she might not like him, she was wise enough to understand that it wasn't always about liking the other person. Sometimes it was about pure animal attraction.

Refusing to think about it, she turned to work. When she'd typed in the wrong figures three times, Gabby admitted she was too tired and too distracted. Time to call it a day.

As she was leaving, she spied Jon at his workbench in the shop. His head was propped on his hand as he studied blueprints. It wasn't until she got closer that she saw his eyes were shut.

He looked oddly boyish. There was something innocent and unguarded in his expression. She felt a weakening in her resistance to him.

"Jon." She put her hand on his shoulder, intending to shake him awake. Instead, it rested there like a caress.

His eyes snapped open.

"You were asleep."

"No, I was, uh, visualizing something on this design." He gestured to the blueprint in front of him then rubbed his eyes.

That gesture dealt a bigger blow to her resistance. She realized it wasn't only animal attraction pulling them together. She took a step backward as if to get away from the knowledge.

She cleared her throat. "I'm heading off now."

He gave her a smile, and she could see his exhaustion.

"Yeah, I should, too." He stood and stretched. The hem of his T-shirt rose as he arched his back and she caught a flash of hard male belly. She looked away, but it was too late. Her mind had committed the image to permanent memory.

And suddenly she knew, for good or bad, she'd never look at Jon the same way again.

Find out what happens next in ONE GOOD REASON, available August 2011 from Harlequin® Superromance®!

Celebrating

Blaze

10 *years of*

red-hot reads

Featuring a special August author lineup of
six fan-favorite authors who have written
for Blaze™ from the beginning!

The Original Sexy Six:

Vicki Lewis Thompson

Tori Carrington

Kimberly Raye

Debbi Rawlins

Julie Leto

Jo Leigh

Pick up all six Blaze™
Special Collectors' Edition titles!

August 2011

Plus visit
HarlequinInsideRomance.com
and click on the Series Excitement Tab
for exclusive Blaze™ 10th Anniversary content!

www.Harlequin.com

HBCELEBRATE0811